Macabres

Quirky Supernatural Tales of Horror

Mick Benderoth

Prepared for publication: 40DayPublishing.com

Cover design: 40DayGraphics.com

Cover art by Alexandra Croix: Alexandracroix.com

Printed in the United States of America

For
my nieces,
Alexandra, Samantha, and Karis
my nephew
Connor,
my granddaughter
Molly
and
my grandson
Griffin
who all continue to enlighten my life.

Acknowledgements

Many thanks to 40 Day Publishing, my astounding *editor* Woody Gimbel, my good friend, *alpha reader* Art Lasky, Thad Rutkowski, whose writer's workshops, "Telling Great Stories", started me on the path to writing prose. My niece Alexandra Croix for allowing me to use her painting, "Ashes to Ashes" for my book cover.

I am also indebted to H.P. Lovecraft and Edgar Allen Poe for imbuing me with the unearthly beauty of horror.

Mick Benderoth, 2022, NYC

"Words have no power to impress the mind without the exquisite horror of their reality."

Edgar Allen Poe

"The oldest and strongest emotion of mankind is fear, and the oldest and strongest kind of fear...is fear of the unknown."

H.P. Lovecraft

"If I can't scare em', I gross em' out."

Stephen King

Contents

M

Shinigami

My divorce. Signed, sealed, delivered. Rid of the bastard. Sitting in my new apartment, free, reborn. My art collection, Pollack, Klee, Jim Dine, a few Atget photos and my prize, a signed Picasso sketch from his artists and models series I bought years ago when I ventured to Mus'ee Picasso in Antibes Art all displayed. Left facing one large, empty white wall. Nothing to hang.

My friend, Geisho Moraki, told me of an up-and-coming Japanese-American woman who just won a Guggenheim. Trained at The Mona Lisa Room, the Louvre. Moishi Suroshi. She took commissions. I called her. Charming, outgoing.

Moishi, "Come on by anytime. I'm always here."

"Noon, tomorrow?"

Moishi, "Cool. I'll steep a fresh pot of green tea. We can chat, do a little bonding, like to know something about people who want my work. See that it gets a good home."

Moishi's studio. Washington Square, Greenwich Village. Uber pulls up to an old brownstone, scaffolding up the face, under renovation. I climb the steps, find Moishi's name, press on the intercom. Press again. Nothing. Press harder. Nothing. Then, the door jars open wide enough for a short, very old Asian woman to stick out her head. She has a squinched, wrinkled face, with long uncombed white hair streaming down her back. No teeth.

Old woman, hoarse voice, screeches, "Intercom don't work. Can't fix. Dunno why. I'm the caretaker. Hafta open the damn door all day. Who you lookin' for?"

Me, "I have an appointment with Moishi Suroshi."

Old woman, "Oh, artist girl, penthouse loft. Take the elevator. If it works. If not, long walk, six flights up steps. Good luck."

Thank god the rattletrap elevator works. I walk down the hall toward an open door, bright daylight streaming in. Smell of oil and turp fills the air like perfume.

I lean in, call, "Moishi, Moishi Suroshi?"

Musical voice echoes, "Maddy Guilford?"

"That's me."

Moishi, "Be right out. Tea's steeping."

The loft is ginormous, half studio, half living space. Moishi's paintings adorn the walls. An abstract expressionist, Moishi's use of color, texture, stunning. A beautiful young woman in paint-splashed Oshkosh overalls comes from behind a large ornate tapestry dividing the space. She carries a tray with a black metal teapot and two cups. She artfully pours the tea.

I lift my cup, take a sip. Hot, hot, hot. Intoxicating. I feel exhilarated, yet relaxed.

Moishi sits on her stool in front of her easel holding a painting in progress. "Geisho told me you have a Klee, a Dine, an original signed Picasso. Thank god no Warhol. A fine place for a painting to live. So, what do you have in mind?"

"I don't have a clue. I have a big white wall, so, something, something…?"

Moishe's studio door creaks open, old crone sticks in her head waving a piece of paper. "Your rent! Your rent! Overdue. You pay or you go." Crone departs, door closes.

Moishe, "Sorry about that." Suddenly the studio turns cold, ice cold. Why? I shiver, continue, "Something that…"

4

Moishi abruptly cuts me off. Her face ashen, her eyes wide, motionless. Then brashly, "Horizontal. Two feet by six, black on white primed canvas, Japanese calligraphy." She snatches her sketch pad, a hunk of charcoal, slashes out twelve Japanese letters. Collapses on her stool, charcoal drops to the floor. Face color returns.

Moishi, reviving, "That was so...so weird. Flashed through my head. My hand, I don't know. It wasn't mine. I just wrote."

Me, awkward, jocular, "Your muse took control."

Moishi, elsewhere, "Something like that."

Me, spell-breaking, "Well, it's extraordinary, bold, stark, commanding. I...I love it. It will fit."

Moishi, resolute, "Finish it tonight."

"Wow. Do you always work so fast?"

Moishi, softly, "Never. Never. A slowpoke." Then curtly, "This piece...demands...fast!"

I take out my checkbook, "Your fee?"

Moishi, now abrupt, "I'll price it when it's finished. Pick it up in the morning. I must get it to where it belongs." Now wearily, "If...if you don't mind, I'm terribly tired."

Me, perplexed, "I...I understand. What's a good time to...?"

"Early, very, very early."

Me, "Nine?"

Moishi, curt, "Earlier. Earlier. Six, seven. It will be ready." She stands. Body trembling. Slips behind the tapestry.

Momentarily motionless. I feel confused, unsettled by Moishi's strange mood swings. Go figure.

Me, in the hall. "Damn!" The elevator's out. I take off my high heels, stumble down six flights, through the front door. Holding my shoes, barefoot, I hail a cab, go home. Hand shaking, I pour some scotch. Too much. Pop a Xanax. Out like a...

5

Morning. Cell alarm pulls me from a deep sleep. Six am. I dress, call Uber.

Moishi's building. I don't ring. I knock. The old woman snarls out. "She not here. She gone."

Me, irritated, "Gone? I came to pick up a painting. She said she'd be waiting."

"Well, she ain't here. Left note."

I grab it. Rip it open.

Moishi's note, *"Couldn't wait. Had it sent."*

Sent? What the hell? Call Uber. Head home.

Back at apartment, Murry behind the counter, "Perfect time Missus…"

Me, irritable. "I'm Miss now. Miss."

Murry, "Big package, Miss. Think the guys will have to take it up when they're free."

Me, more irritated, "Hell with that! If the damn thing's not in my apartment immediately I'll…"

Murry "Ok, ok. I'll…I'll take it up for you."

My apartment. More Xanax. Scotch chaser. This is way, way off normal. Not new normal. Weird normal.

Doorbell. Murry with the painting. Wrapped haphazardly in linen. Linen? I tip Murry. He leaves. I unwrap. There it is. On canvas. Moishi's sketch, completed. Mesmerizing. Need to get it hung immediately. Measure once, measure twice. My father, a carpenter. Use three twenty-pound hooks. Unframed, no wire. Hang it just the way it is. Problem solved, artfully. Owns the wall.

Someone has to see it. I spontaneously invite Geisho, his wife Allison, Mary Ann, my paralegal, and Randall, right and left-hand man, over to see my acquisition.

Later, they all show. Visitors all present, the painting draped in the linen.

Me, unveiling. "Ta dah!'" I whisk off the drape.

Gasps, praise from Allison. Mary Ann, paralegal, Randall.

Me, "What about you Geisho? You aren't saying anything."

Geisho, derisive, laughing, "Damn! She painted *that?* It's a laugh riot. What did you pay?"

I snap, "What are you talking about? What's so damn funny?""

Geisho, "Your painting. The word is *Shinigami.* Japanese demon, death bringer. Myth says his name should never be written. Writing his name frees him. Fairy tale. She pulled a fast one."

Guests all join Geisho laughing. At my painting. At me. I'm pissed. Humiliated. Sensing my displeasure, they leave. I sit facing... *Shinigami,* feeling like a fool. Two glasses of wine, a Xanax.

Later, in bed watching the late news. On the screen, an ambulance, police, crowd of onlookers, the Hudson waterfront. Some guy talking. TV guy, "I was jogging. Saw something wedged between the rocks. Checked it out. Dead body...no *bleeping* head."

TV reporter grimly faces the camera. "Investigators identified the body as Moishi Suroshi, a local artist. Head ripped off. Apparent macabre murder."

Freaked, I grapple for the remote. Kill the TV. Moishi. Murdered. Slaughtered. Why? More Xanax. Down for the count. Nightmare. Image flashes. Geisho laughing. All of them laughing. At my painting. Big faces. Grotesque.

Later, Geisho's apartment door. I stand wearing a shower curtain, slit cut out for my head. A gleaming sharp meat clever in my hand. I knock. Geisho answers.

"Maddy, what are you...?" Never finishes.

Swish! Geisho's head thumps to the floor. Blood spurts, spurts, spurts from his neck stub with each fading heartbeat. Splashes the ceiling. His trunk collapses in the pool of blood.

Allison runs from the kitchen. She screams. *Swish! Thump.* Two heads. Husband and wife, facing each other on the floor.

7

Dead of night. Walking down an alley. Throws cleaver into a dumpster along with blood-drenched shower curtain.

Another nightmare. I sit up quaking in my bed. Sweat running down my face. Dash to kitchen, pour a stiff scotch. Drink it down. Gotta cut back on the drinking. Shower. Go to the office. The place in chaos.

Randall, tears stream down his face. "He's dead. Both dead. Geisho and Allison. Horrible. Horrible."

Randall shoves *Daily News* into my hand. Front page headline, "Lawyer and Wife Beheaded."

Me. Dead faint. Flashbacks. Blood. Blood. More blood…everywhere. Regain consciousness. Confused. Staff surrounds my chair. We commiserate over our horrid loss. I go home. Scotch. Xanax.

Me. Morning, hung over, reach for coffee, seated at my marble bistro table. Can't process. Moishi, Geisho, Allison. Knocking over my cup and table, I shake out of control. My head snaps to the painting. Cold sweat. Mind blanks.

Unearthly voice. "Kill them, kill them all."

I black out. Another nightmare. Again.

Randal's gym. Men's locker room. He's putting on workout clothes. I'm there.

Randal, shocked, "Maddy? How the hell did you…?"

Cleaver. *Swish! Thump.*

Black out. Wake up on my bedroom floor. Blood covered. No dream. Am I the killer? The painting? Shinigami? Death bringer? Me?

Not possible. I rush into the living room. Grab letter opener from my desk. *Slash! Slash! Slash! Rip* the painting to shreds. Pull it off the wall. On the floor. Kick it! Kick it…maniacally. *Smash* the frame. Carry it to the utility room. Jam it down the incinerator chute. What in god's name should I do now? I go back to my apartment. Panic attack!

Me, "Dear God!" The painting! Back on my wall. Drop into a chair. Mental whiteout.

Mary Ann's apartment. I hide around the corner. She exits dressed for work. Sneakers on, dress shoes in hand, New York style. I turn the corner. Walk quickly behind her. She hears. Turns.

"Maddy?"

Swish! Thump. Roll.

My apartment. Still seated. Eyes locked on the painting. Slowly, slowly, an indescribable monster materializes. *Shinigami.*

Shinigami speaks, *"Kill... Kill...you. Kill you."*

Entranced. I stroll zombie-like to the kitchen. Take butcher knife from drawer. Automatically draw it across sharpening steel. Return to *Shinigami.*

Shinigami's voice repeating, *"Kill you, kill, kill. You."*

Knife pursed. I methodically slit my throat. Blood gushes. Hit the floor. Barely alive. Foggy eyed.

Apartment door opens. Old Japanese crone steps over my body, smiling toothlessly.

Takes painting off the wall.

Japanese crone, last words, to the painting. "Finished. We go now." She drags Shinigami out the door.

My last breath gurgles.

M

Broom Straws

Tap! Tap! Tap! of the Conductor's baton as Deborah Allen, twenty-six-year-old beloved middle school music teacher, stands proudly in a tuxedo leading the Reyker School's yearly orchestra recital. The students dressed neat as a pin. Recital begins. A few bleeps! Squeaks! Squawks! Tune up. Baton raised, the orchestra leaps into the theme from Star Wars. Comes off hitchless. Parents, standing ovation. Deborah gestures. Her well-dressed musicians stand, bow. A boy and girl scamper onstage, present Deborah a bouquet. More applause.

Deborah at après recital gathering, chats with adoring parents. A tall, thin, black suited man pushes through the crowd, walks directly to Deborah, hands a business card. Blandly, "I'm Parnell Tubman. I represent The Old Providence Bank of New York. Our president, Mr. Willowy requests a meeting regarding pressing family financial matters.

Deborah, "What exactly does that mean?"

Tubman, "I'm not at liberty to say more. Mr. Willowy asks that you call, set up a meeting at your earliest convenience. Nice meeting you, Miss Allen."

Tubman spins on his heels, scutters away. Deborah scans the card quizzically. Shrugs.

Saturday morning. A black limousine pulls up as Deborah stands curbside, dressed in a navy-blue business suit, sensible black shoes. The driver exits, walks to, opens rear door, arm gestures. Deborah slides in. The limo pulls up to The Old

13

Providence Bank. Unimpressive, small weather-beaten building. Tubman escorts Deborah inside.

Mr. Willowy, a plump, older man in a three-piece tweed suit, tiny pince-nez glasses. Gets up from behind an old well-worn oak desk. Skitters around to Deborah. Holds out his hand.

Willowy, "Miss Allen, I am Baxter Willowy president of the bank. We've had a dickens of a time locating you."

Tubman, hovering close to Willowy. "Yes, yes. Almost a year."

Mr. Willowy nods to Tubman, who disappears, returns with an aged crude wooden chest. Places it on the coffee table in front of the leather couch.

Deborah, "I must say I am a bit skeptical. I have never heard of your bank. I couldn't even find it with an internet search."

Willowy, smiles. "We are a specialty bank. We cater to the needs of a very, um, shall we say, specific... clientele, Miss Allen."

She nods. "Please call me Deborah."

Willowy, "Ah, yes, then, Deborah it is. You may proceed Parnell."

He opens the box, takes great care unfolding a dusty parchment.

Willowy, "This may sound strange, Deborah, but that is the Last Will and Testament of your distant relative, Eliza Allen."

Deborah, "I don't recall the name."

Willowy, "Likely not. Eliza died in 1648 in Salem, Massachusetts. We've managed the money for 555 years, per her instructions. We've amassed quite a tidy sum. Eliza leaves her entire fortune to you."

Tubman, nudging, "Ten million smackaroos."

Deborah stands, abruptly shaken, "Is...is this for real?"

Mr. Willowy, "Oh Yes. We have the full amount in the bank vault if you'd like to see it."

Deborah, dizzy at the revelation, "No. Maybe later. Could I have a glass of water?"

Mr. Willowy, "Parnell, if you please." Parnell dashes out, returns with a cold bottle of Avian.

Parnell Tubman, "One could live in luxury on the interest alone..."

Willowy, "Parnell, enough. The other items, please. Just open the box."

Parnell Tubman takes out a ragged envelope and a parcel wrapped in frayed, age-stained muslin. Closes the box, places objects on top. Unwraps the cloth parcel, spilling what appears to be, five old, yellowed sticks onto the box.

Deborah, "What...?"

Tubman, pertly, "Broom straws."

Deborah, "From a broom?"

Tubman, "A very, very old one, hand made from a tree bough avec straws."

Willowy, "One caveat. Unusual. Carefully delineated in her will. You must carry out Eliza's wishes, locating the last remaining descendants of the jury that found her guilty of...witchcraft. All five descendants are named, except for one."

Deborah jaw drops. "Eliza Allen was a witch?"

Willowy, "Accused."

Tubman, "After all, they say there is no such thing as witches."

Willowy gives Tubman a hard eye. "And...as I was saying, you must also find the last living descendant of Reverend Judge Manchin Ambrose, the judge who pronounced her death sentence..."

Parnell Tubman, overstepping, "Hung by the neck until...dead."

Willowy, "Parnell, your room."

Parnell sulks off.

Deborah, "Actually hanged for being a witch? Barbaric."

Tubman, shouting from the back, "The word 'Witch' burned in her forehead."

Willowy, shouting at Tubman, "And close the door. Please. Now, where was I? Oh, there is one troubling item. The only eyewitness who accused Eliza was an unknown, unnamed young woman. Difficult to find. At any rate, when you find each of the descendants, you are to have them read Eliza's prayer of apparent forgiveness."

He takes the envelope, pulls out smaller parchment, unwraps, then reads:

> *"To those who stood*
> *and watched that day.*
> *I send this prayer from my heart*
> *to you and blood kin.*
> *May this gift*
> *of a straw from my broom*
> *fulfill this prayer*
> *from my grave.*
> *Break the straw."*

Deborah, apprehensively, "Break the straw?"

Willowy, "No idea. No explanation. I prepared a document to be signed, verifying Eliza's wishes are carried out after you find and explain the details to each descendant. You'll surely be facing their dubious surprise and reticence. As an incentive for them to cooperate, offer them the sum of twenty-five-thousand dollars. That's it. To assist you in finding the descendants here's the card of a genealogist, Jason Miller. Well known, high standing."

Deborah, "What about this unknown, unnamed, mystery woman?"

Willowy frowns, "Unfortunately, if unfound, you receive nary a cent."

16

Deborah, skeptical, "This is so ridiculous. A child's game. No hope of winning."

Willowy, "You have the right to disown the will. You can walk away."

Tubman, yelling out...again, "For that money, I'd give it the old college try, honey."

Willowy, outraged, "Parnell! Enough!"

Deborah, "So, the money is mine if I fulfill this unusual quest."

Willowy, "Yes. The decision is up to you, Deborah. Up to you."

Deborah, "What the heck. In for a penny..."

Tubman, again, "...in for ten million...bucks."

Willowy, "Parnell, the contract!" To Deborah, "Just sign this legal agreement. I'll notarize."

Parnell Tubman scutters out with the document, places it before Deborah, hands her a quill pen. "Careful. Real ink smudges."

Deborah takes a deep breath, signs.

Willowy, "Very well. I have opened a private account providing you a generous amount for expenses. That's about it. We will keep her will and the funds in the vault."

Tubman places the bank documents, will, and the broom straws, back in the box. "I'll take it out to the limousine for you Deborah."

Mr. Willowy holds out his hand to Deborah. "Please keep in touch. We are at your service. Good luck."

Deborah into the limo, box at her side. Afraid to handle it. Gives in, puts hands on her...destiny?

Later, Deborah sits in a bar, nurses a double scotch. She mutters, "I have some ancient relative accused of being a...a witch. What are witches anyway? A Halloween costume she wore in a fifth-grade party...black cape and a plastic pointed hat. Dumb. But still?"

Deborah goes to library for research. Reads from a tome, mumbles, *"Witches are not immortal, have no superhuman powers, can be tortured, killed like any human.* But another book says *Witches can cast spells and curses, their spirits can arise from their graves, eternally."* Hmm.

Deborah, "I can't believe I've signed up for this. But I did. First task, track down this genealogist, Jason Miller" She dials his card number. No answer.

A message, "You have reached the answering…"

Finally, a male voice answers, "Hello, hello?"

Deborah, "Jason Miller?"

Jason, "Yes, who is…"

Deborah, ignoring his question, "Jason, Want a job?"

Deborah and Jason Miller at the coffee shop. Deborah explains, then asks, "Way weird right?"

Jason, "Never had a case like this, for sure."

Deborah, "If you pull this off, I'll give you a chunk of my fortune, say a full half-million."

Jason. Speechless. Nervously pops a cherry lozenge in his mouth. Couple of sucks. Clears his throat, "Well, that's a handsome fee."

Deborah, "So?"

Smiling, sucking, "I'm hired."

They shake heartily. She reaches into her knapsack, pulls out a thick wad of hundred-dollar bills, slaps them in his hands. "Five grand, egg money. Should keep you going for a while."

Jason pops another lozenge, says "Nervous habit. My throat gets dry. Want one?"

Deborah, "Why not." He gives. She pops. Both laugh.

Deborah. Late night bubble bath, her apartment bathroom. A glass of scotch rests precariously on tub edge. She takes a gulp, thinking of all the things money can bring: Upscale apartment, a car that runs, and money to travel— never been out of the country. The world is my oyster. Another scotch. Then, strange stillness. Room ice cold. Dense fog. She shivers. Stands. Feels for her terry cloth purple robe. Grabs, puts it on. Image shimmers in the fog. What the hell?

Vision, a young woman's hand viciously stabs the air. She points at a terrified peasant woman running down a cobblestone street. Harsh voice, the Accuser, *"It's her! It's her! I saw it all, I saw it all. Horrible things. I saw it all. Eliza Allen is a witch. I swear on the Holy Bible…she's a witch."*

Vision grows. Eliza Allen, tied, spread eagle against a stone wall. Crazed villagers hurl stones. She's hit, again, again, again, deep cuts. Blood trickles down her face. Eliza Allen pleads, screams, *"No! No! No!"* Eliza tied in the dunking stool. Plunged under water, again and again. Raised, gasping for air. *"Lies, all lies! I am not a witch."*

Vision shifts. Three hate-faced jurors hiss, *"Guilty! Guilty! Guilty!"*

Vision narrows, massive face grins, deep velvet voice. Words slide from his fat lips. *"I, Judge Manchin Ambrose, sentence Eliza Allen to die, to be hung by the neck…until dead."* Judge Ambrose bangs his gavel, *Slam! Slam! Slam!*

Vision fades. Room clears. Deborah, dazed, stands in the tub, arms held tightly around her waist, face ashen, teeth chatter, lips quiver. Shakes her head to clear. Grabs scotch. Shoots it. Horrid vision. She will keep it too herself.

Jason's office, setting up a trip to Salem. Deborah feigns a cough, "Got any more lozenges?"

Jason points to his desk, "Top drawer."

She goes, opens, laughs loud. The drawer overflows with lozenge boxes. "You've got a serious jones going here." Deborah chuckles, "Get your butt to LA."

Jason, "Los Angeles?"

Deborah, "Lozenges Anonymous." They share hardy laughs.

Deborah at school teaching her beloved music students. "Ok, all, I want you to…"

She becomes dizzy. Flops into her chair. Children disappear.

Another vision. A wooden beam raised by poles. Red hot branding iron pressed hard against Eliza's brow. Gagged, a muted scream of agony. Sizzle of burning flesh. Smoking word "WITCH" forever embossed. Flop! A thick-noosed rope drops, settles roughly around Eliza's scrawny neck. Drawn tight. Judge Ambrose pull lever. Trap door open. Eliza drops. Swoosh! Crack! Neck broken. Dead. She sways beneath the gallows. Body becomes still. Speaks. Dull echo. Gallows voice, *"Read my prayer. Snap the straw. I will be with you, with you, snap the straw."*

Vision fades into the ether. Deborah, shaken. Sits, tears flowing. Children afraid. Another secret vision.

Deborah at Jason's office next morning. Befuddled, groggy, withdrawn.

Jason, concerned, "Are you ok? You look…"

Deborah, lying, "Mexican takeout. Didn't agree. Couldn't keep anything down. Worst is over." Takes a deep breath. "What have you got?"

Jason, upbeat, "Located a possible juror's descendant. Allison Campbell, Wall Street bigwig. VP of Microsoft Stock sales. She's…she's not a definite. We'll know one way or another when we question her. I'll call, set up…"

Deborah, her mind far away, feels Eliza's power. Replies curtly, "No. No. I will make the call. I'll know the truth when I gaze in her eyes. I will do this by myself."

Jason, "Can I at least accompany you to the market. Moral support."

Deborah, as if in a trance, "Yes. You can come along. No interference. Me. Alone."

Jason, "Well, if that's the way you…"

Deborah in a harsh voice, not her own, "The only way."

Floor of the stock exchange. Deborah pulls Jason as they weave through the chaotic screaming throng barking out stock orders.

Deborah screams at a security guard, "I'm looking for Allison Campbell."

Security guard points, "She just ducked into the ladies' room. Over there, around that corner."

Deborah, "Thanks."

Jason and Deborah navigate the crowd.

Jason, "We'll wait till she comes out. You can suggest meeting in her office."

Deborah, "No. Right now. Right here. Myself." She heads for the Ladies' room.

Jason gently takes her arm. "Deborah, this isn't proper. Just wait until she…"

Deborah pulls away gruffly. Head snaps. Faces Jason. Eyes wide. Face stern. A different Deborah, sharp, harsh whisper, "You will wait here until the deed is done."

She stalks into the woman's room, leaving Jason discombobulated.

Deborah, "Allison?"

Deborah leans against the Ladies' room door. Toilet flushes. Tall, portly blonde exits a stall. Starts for the exit. Deborah blocks her way. Does not move.

Allison, "Excuse me. Please move out of my way."

Deborah does not budge.

Allison reddens, "Please don't make me call security."

Deborah, low growl, "That will not be necessary. I am Deborah Allen. We spoke."

Allison cools a bit. Still feels situation awkward, "Oh, yes. Something about a family…"

Deborah, "Inheritance. Money. Money for signing a document."

Allison, "Maybe we should go into my office to…"

Deborah, abruptly: "No. We will finish here."

Allison, "A little unusual, but sure. I…I never caught your name?"

Deborah, eyes glazed: *"Eliza. Call me Eliza."*

Allison, I thought your name was Deborah Allen?

Deborah growls. *"It is. I don't know what I was thinking."*

Allison, unsteady, "Alright, Deborah, or Eliza. So, what's this about? You, ah, said something about money."

Deborah hands Allison the document. Speaks in a voice not her own. *"When thee makest thy mark on the paper, thee will be compensated."*

Alison, shaken at the strange language and voice, scans the document, "Twenty-five thousand dollars? Where…"

Deborah cuts her off, *"Family inheritance."*

Allison commanding. "I have little time. So get on with…"

Deborah shoves out the check. Allison grabs it. Deborah does not release. A bizarre moment, uncomfortable tug of war. Allison releases. Deborah hands her the document to sign.

Deborah, *"Sign first. Then you will get what's coming to you."*

Apparition. Eliza, noosed, hanging from a thick hemp rope.

Allison screams, freaks, horrified, shaking, "My…my God…what…who…"

Eliza, *"I be thy benefactor to repay you for deeds done."* She screeches, *"My prayer! Give her my prayer! Read my prayer!"*

Ladies' room turns ice cold. Mirrors frost. Allison sees her breath. Shivers. Mind boggled.

Eliza's voice, *"Read my prayer. Now!"*

Deborah hands Allison Eliza's prayer. "Do what she says. Read it."

Allison shivers fearfully, *"To…to…those who stood and watched that day…"*

Jason paces outside the women's room. Thinks. "Deborah's been gone a long time. Should I go in? No.

Deborah was adamant. She will do this alone. I'll just hang out."

Allison finishing the prayer, *"…May this…this gift of a straw from my broom fulfill my prayer from my grave."*

Deborah, icily, "Now you will receive what you deserve."

Eliza's voice hisses, *"Break thy straw. Break it now!"*

Deborah holds up the straw in front of Allison.

Allison, unglued, "What is all this …it can't be happening. I don't know how you are doing this but…"

Deborah breaks the broom straw. *Snap! Rrrrrrup! Crack!* Allison, noosed, jerked, hung. *Push! Push! Push!* Gruesome sounds of her vertebrae pulling apart. Her eyes bulge, mouth open, tongue flopped out. Dead.

Eliza's voice to Deborah, "Thou goest forth to the next. Find them all." Eliza's rasping words fade. Her image dissipates, leaves a smoky stench.

Jason, outside the bathroom door, still pacing, glances at his watch. Deborah bursts out the door, smiling, waving the signed contract.

Jason, "How did it go?"

Deborah, bubbly, "Piece a cake. Met her, waved the check in her face. Signed *tout suite*. Shook hands. One jurist down two to go."

She grabs Jason's hand, pulls him into the cacophonous stock market mob.

Deborah and Jason. His office. He's on the verge of bursting out laughing, "Second juror, if you can believe it, *Miss Universe, 1960*. Andrea Manella. Now runs a spa in Newport beach."

Deborah "Who's the last one?"

Jason hands her the fax.

Deborah, surprised, "A police Chief?"

Jason: "Landford Brently, Massachusetts born and bred. Moved to New York twenty years ago. Worked his way up from rookie to Chief. He works out of 87th Precinct in Brooklyn."

Deborah stands before Police Chief Landford Brently, Police Chief, New York City's 87th Precinct.

Deborah, gravel-voiced, "A few issues then, you will get what you deserve."

Eliza slowly materializes. Chief sees the ghastly vision, loses it. Starts screaming. *Snap! Swoosh! Crack! Done.*

Deborah trains to Newport. Taxi to the *Wonderspa.* Inside finds Andrea Manella, former Miss Universe's cabana.

Deborah, cold as ice, explains, then says, "Sign here. You will get what you deserve." Manella signs. Eliza appears, right on time. *Scream. Snap! Whoosh! Crack! Fait accompli.*

Jason's office. On cell with Deborah. Visibly upset.

Deborah, "Any news from our Salem guy? The Judge? Our Mystery Girl?"

Jason, distraught, lying, "Yes. Some papers just needed processing. He'll fax them ASAP."

Deborah, "Call me."

Jason, "Of course." He slumps in his chair, scanning already faxed documents. Opens his briefcase, takes out a sheaf of papers. Holds them too long. Deep breath. Opens his desk drawer, puts the documents in the drawer, closes, locks. Sits. Near catatonic.

Next morning. Jason's office. Deborah enters, fresh and ready. Scans room. No Jason. Deborah, "Jason, Jason?"

"In the den."

Deborah strolls in. Jason, kneeling at the fireplace, stacking twigs. Deborah takes off her coat, flings it on the couch. "A fire. How nice and cozy. Getting chilly outside."

Jason, mumbles, "Winter."

Deborah, "You OK. Look a bit …"

Jason, "Late night. I'm fine, fine."

Deborah, "Get the goods?"

Jason, "Waiting for me when I got here."

The room starts to fill with smoke. Deborah starts coughing.

Jason, "I...I forgot to open the flue."

Deborah coughs harder, "I'm gonna get a lozenge from your desk." She spins on her heel. Rushes out.

Jason's office. Deborah surprised to find the desk drawer locked. No problem. Jimmies it with a letter opener. Finds documents. Reads. Blanches. Shock and awe. Rages into the den, catches Jason burning documents in the fireplace.

Deborah, "You bastard. Burning evidence. Too late. I read the originals." Screams, "Trying to escape your fate, destroying proof of who you are. Coward!"

Jason stands, shattered, "No, no. You have it wrong. I...I was burning these...because of what they revealed..."

She yanks the charred documents from his hand.

Jason emotionally, "...about you."

Deborah reads. Her face turns whiter than white. She wobbles, terror in her eyes, drops to the couch.

Deborah, "My...my God, it's me. The mystery woman. Eliza's own daughter turned her in. I'm her last living descendant."

Jason sits beside her. "And I'm the last descendant of Manchin Ambrose...the hanging judge."

Deborah jumps up, raving, pacing. "I carried out Eliza's vengeance. Murdered them. Innocent people. I don't deserve to live." She faces Jason, "You killed no one. Just a victim of lincage."

Jason stands, "You were possessed. Powerless. You didn't kill. She did."

Deborah, tears welling, "I only have two broom straws left. One for..."

Jason, "...each of us."

Deborah, "I will not, cannot do this. It stops here."

A rasping voice reverberates, *"And just how dost thou plan to escape me, granddaughter?"* They spin around to see Eliza's rancid,

25

decaying body in filthy tatters. Bare bones show through rotted flesh.

"Fear not. my child. Thou hast done well, revealing my daughter's treachery. She will burn in hell. Thee I will spare." Eliza points a ragged finger at Jason.

Eliza, *"This animal, last kin of Reverend Manchin Ambrose, who strangled life from me, must pay. Finish it. Now!"*

Deborah, "I will not!"

Eliza, *"You would do best to reconsider."*

Deborah, "No, you horrid creature. I will not kill another innocent for your personal revenge."

Eliza, *"So be it. You have chosen your fate."* Eliza extends her arm. The broom straws vanish from Deborah's hand, reappear in Eliza's fist. Snap! Snap Swoosh! Swoosh! Crack! Crack! Deborah and Jason, noosed, yanked, hung. Both dead.

Eliza, self-satisfied, *"If thee desireth a thing done right, thee must do it thy self."* Fades away, cackling. Deborah and Jason swing, side by side, human pendulums. On the floor beneath their dangling feet, two broom straws, broken.

M

Catharsis

"**W**ilma, will you get off this 'find me a man' kick. One abusive marriage and divorce, another Mr. Right, who cheated on me forever. No more unfaithful men!" Annie Rhodes, a slim thirty-something woman. Bluetooth in her ear, paces, smokes, dresses for work, sister on the phone. She takes another drag, exhales raggedly.

Wilma, "Are you smoking?"

Annie, "No, I quit—You know that."

Wilma, "People aren't meant to live alone. Cuts years off your life. You gotta see my therapist about this. She saved my marriage."

Annie, "For a year. Then he took off with your best friend."

Wilma, "Whatever. Please. For me. Try. I'll text you her number."

Annie, "Whatever, whatever. I'm late. Gotta leave. I'll call you from the cab."

Annie misbuttons her suit jacket, "Arrrrg! Shit! Dammit!"

Out on the cold, rainy street, she hails a cab. One pulls over. A beefy guy rushes up in front of her.

Beefy, "My ride, tootsie. I was hailing before you got here."

Annie, "Hell you were. He saw me first."

Annie moves in front of him, opens door. Beefy guy shoves her away, slides into cab.

Beefy, "Next time little girl."

Annie, "Ladies first, jerk. Didn't your mother teach you that?"

Beefy, Guy, "Chivalry's dead, babe." Slams the door. Drives off.

Annie yelling after, "Creep!" She frowns, hails again.

Thankfully, doesn't have a long wait—a minor miracle on a rainy day. Gives the driver the address, then relaxes, dials her sister. Ten minutes later, she exits the cab and races up to her building entrance, still gabbing on the cell with Wilma.

Annie, "Lunch later. You pick—"

She collides with a tall blond-haired guy, sunglasses, tailored Italian suit, head buried in his newspaper. Phone and newspaper go flying.

Blond man, "Damn you girly. Watch it!"

Annie, "Well if you pulled your head out of your damn paper, you'd see where you're going."

Blond man, "Screw you bitch."

Annie, "That'll never happen. Screw yourself, bastard."

She scoops up her phone, pushes past him. He flips her the bird. She gives it back, double, hurries to the elevator, repeatedly jabs the call button. She stands, impatient, foot tapping,

The door slides open. "Finally!" she says, loud enough for all to hear.

Two guys block the front. Some twit raises his hand halting her.

Twit, "Hold it tootsie. No time to make room. Bye-bye." The doors close.

Annie, under her breath, "Assholes."

She catches the next elevator and dashes into her office, a barely acceptable ten minutes late. Spends the next two hours dealing with emergencies and putting out fires.

Finally, she mutters to herself, "I need coffee, a smoke and more coffee. Okay, Annie, get yourself to the break room."

Annie waits for the coffee to brew, in the happily empty break room. She ignores the NO SMOKING Sign and lights up. Just as she takes the first relaxing puff, a doughy butterball of a guy strolls in.

Butterball, "No smoking Little Orphan Annie. Bad for your,..ur..." Hesitates. Gestures at her breasts, "...chest."

Annie, "Get lost, Donald. You pig."

He leaves, smirking.

Lisa, a colleague walks in catching the tail end of the conversation, pipes up. "You got that right. Lard Butt hits on every woman in the office."

Annie takes a last puff. Dunks butt under sink water. Tosses into trash.

Lisa, "Thought you quit?"

Annie, "I did until Wilma forced me into therapy."

Lisa, "Been there, done that. Good luck."

The rest of the day passes in a blur of phone calls, meetings, and paperwork. Annie checks her watch, mutters, "Almost six, I'd like to blow off the friggin' therapist, but Wilma would never forgive me."

She throws on her jacket and heads out to the street. It's a little after the worst of the rush hour, so catching a cab isn't a major ordeal. By six thirty, she's sitting in the therapist's office.

Annie, "The hell with this couch shit."

Therapist, Lidia Marks, "So, we're here for anger management?"

Annie, wide-eyed, "We?"

Lidia, "Just a figure of..."

Annie, seething, "My anger's doing just fine. I need help with pushy moronic male management."

Lidia, "Why don't we take a deep breath. In. Out. Calm down and..."

Annie explodes, "Calm down? Is that all you got! Breathing exercises. The hell with this, we're done here."

Annie storms out. Slams the door.

Back home, Annie, teeth gnashing, drenched in sweat, manically pedals her exercise bike in a race to nowhere. Jumps off, takes a molten shower, bathroom a steam-choked sauna. Thoroughly broiled, hops out, grabs a towel. The shower's done little to lower her temper. She wipes the mirror so hard she knocks shampoo and pill bottles everywhere. Stops wiping, settles down, starts flossing.

Annie, "Now what?" she growls. Something's not right. She stops flossing. Her face shimmers with a strange yellow-green glow. She feels dizzy. Leans against the wall to steady herself. Gags. Dry heaves. Grabs her chest with both hands. A sinewy, gnarled, puce hand pushes out between her fingers. Annie freaks, trembles. Another hand appears...then a horrid nonhuman nude form steps out of her body. Its head covered with long, tangled, Medusa-like hair, hanging over its bony shoulders and withered, sagging breasts. A bizarre visage, a distorted female figure, eyes black as coal.

"Hello, Annie," emanates from a gash of a mouth.

Annie, in a cold sweat, eyes shut tight, says to herself, "This is a nightmare, Annie. Wake up." She opens her eyes. The horrid visage still before her.

Visage, "No dream, very, very real."

Annie trembling, "Wha...what in God's name are...are you?"

Visage's raspy voice, "I am you, Annie. I come from you. I am your Hate."

Annie, "I...I don't *hate* anybody."

Visage, "Don't lie to yourself. Don't lie to me. You hate men. Admit it. Too many have disappointed you, slighted you, used you. They disgust you. I am here to help. You will be pleased. We are one. We are one. We are one."

The wretched, puce form slides back inside Annie's body, voice reverberates, fades.

Annie's splashes cold water on her face, slumps catatonic on the toilet seat.

Annie shakes it off, lies to herself, "I just need a good night's sleep. That's all."

She sleeps soundly, dreamlessly. Alarm goes off at 7:30. She wakes refreshed, ready for the day racing with the rats. She pauses, recalls last night's weirdness. Puzzled.

Annie, to herself, "Had to be a nightmare. I don't hate all men, just the 99% who are sexist dogs." She dismisses it all with a little laugh, settles into the workday routine.

Back at work. Donald, the beefy sexist pig, passes her desk, "Lookin' hot today, Annie babes. Way hot." He reaches out, touches her face, "Ouchy, ouch! Too hot. I'm going to the John, Baby Cakes. Wanna join me?"

Annie, "Get out of my sight, idiot. How many times do I have to say NO, before it sinks in?"

He walks away smirking. Heads to bathroom.

Beefy Donald, pissing at a urinal. Hears door squeak. Looks over his shoulder, still pissing. Door creeps open. He sees Annie walk in, zombie-like.

Beefy Donald, "Well now, Annie Oakley. Guess our time has come." He finishes up, faces her fully. His dick dangling out of his fly. "I'll make it easy. Just kneel and enjoy."

Annie frozen. Visage steps out of her.

Beefy Donald, freaked, "What the hell is…" He never finishes.

The visage points. Donald's body bursts into flame. Skin sizzles. Donald screams in anguish. …then fades, ceases to exist. Hate fulfilled.

Visage reenters Annie, voice echoes, "We won. We won. We will always win."

Strange, Annie feels more satisfied than shocked. Fixes her lipstick in men's room mirror. Smiles broadly. Winks at herself. Struts out. The rest of the day passes in a blur, until Annie finds herself heading home. She punches the elevator call button and waits, almost patiently, until the elevator door opens, it's crowded. She recognizes the twit and a few of the others.

Twit's raises his hand to block her again, Visage steps out, points. Men erupt in flames. Scream! Sizzle! Scream! Gone.

Annie smiles, savors the evil spectacle, "Well done."

She enters the empty elevator. Doors close, she enjoys a quiet ride to the lobby.

Annie, to herself, "It's a lovely day. I've got a dinner date with Wilma. It's not far, I think I'm going to walk."

Blissful, she strolls along the avenue, enjoying the fair weather. She passes a barbershop. Cat calls, wolf whistles sail through the shop's open door, all aimed at Annie, darkening her mood. She comes to a dead stop. Enters the barbershop. Stands transfixed. The customers neck-jerk, leer, and drool.

Vinnie, front chair, calls out, "Take a seat sweetheart. Geordie is free next. He's great with chicks. Plant your cute little tush on the bench."

Annie, "I prefer to stand." Visage steps out. Points. Mens' hair and clothing burst into flame. Total immolation. Gone. Visage withdraws. Annie, deeply satisfied, smiles, moves on to dinner with her sister.

Wilma, "You look ravishing sis. You score big time or what?"

Annie, "Yes. Scored…big time."

Wilma, "My therapist said you stormed out."

Annie, "I don't need therapy. I have all the help I need. Gotta run. Work."

Wilma eyes her sister quizzically, "Huh? Shortest dinner ever. What's wrong?"

Annie dashes out, no answer other than a beatific smile. Heads to the subway almost skipping down the stairs. With a sprint she just squeezes through the closing subway car doors. She stands, holding a pole in a packed subway. A man, hidden by his newspaper brushes her back.

Annie, "Do you mind giving me some breathing room?"
The man lowers his paper. It's the blond.
Blond, "Well, well. The little bitch again."
Annie, "And the big…bastard. Just keep your distance."
Blond, "No problem honey. She-wolves not my type."
Annie, "Innocent secretaries your prey?"
Blond, "You are a vicious witch."

Annie, enraged, raises her arm to nail him. Subway lurches. She falls to the floor. Her misandric Visage seeps out of her body, points a deadly finger, targets the blond.

Annie, "I have no control."
Blond, "Nor do I."

Annie is shocked when a puce Visage with vestigial male sex organs oozes out of his body. The blond's grotesque wraith lifts its arm, points at Annie. Bizarre standoff. Annie and blond make eye contact. Deep atavistic, primal human bond overtakes them. Male and female. Together. The blond instinctively leaps in front of Annie, shielding her. She reaches out, impulsively grabs his leg, pulling him out of her Visage's deadly path.

The blond reaches out his hand to help Annie up. She responds, accepts his helpful grasp. He pulls her up. They stand side by side. Hand in hand. Both Visages screech as the mates face their creations, hands locked. The Visages, Misandry and Misogyny, convulse violently, face off, point, howl, flame, ephemerate each other in a blinding flash. The subway car is total screaming chaos. Annie and the blond man are separated in the confusion as the train lurches into the next stop. The doors open and disgorge a stampede. Annie dazedly finds her way home.

Annie, "Sleep I just wanna sleep."

Annie awakens from what feels like a long nightmare. The day is bright, fresh, full of hope. She finds herself whistling a merry little tune as she makes her way to the office. Outside the building she pauses to enjoy the fresh air for a few more moments. This results in a collision with a man buried in his newspaper. He peeks around the paper. It's the blond, smiling.

Blond, "Pardon me, ma'am." He opens the door. "Ladies first."

Annie, demurely, "Thank you, kind sir. I guess chivalry isn't dead."

Blond, "Not as far as my mom was concerned." Holds out his hand. "Mark Kenner, tenth floor, Random House. You?"

They shake. "Annie Rhodes. Eighth floor. Wayland Management."

Mark, "Pleased to meet you, Annie Rhodes."

Annie, cheerful, "Pleasure's all mine, Mark Kenner."

Annie and Mark enter the building chatting like old friends.

Catharsis.

M

Miasma

Miasma, an atavistic malodorous power of unknown origin, spuming plaque on unatoned murders… and those engrossed."

Falling, falling, falling. It all passes before your eyes, flickering like an old black-and-white horror movie. Living it, agonizing yet enjoying the memory.

Your family stands at Mark's grave, your identical twin brother. A yearly birthday ritual for the last ten years. A strange odor hovers, stronger every year. Only you smell it. Your secret. They have their own. Mother speaks lovingly to Mark's earthly mound. You're uncomfortable at this annual ceremony.

Your mother kneels, kisses Mark's gravestone, whispers too sweetly, "Mark, my darling, not a day goes by that I…we…don't think of you. This year you are a man. Twenty-one. Here are presents I…we…your family brought for you."

You watch her unwrap each gift placing them on Mark's grave describing each as if he were there…alive. A yellow toy school bus, a jar of black jellybeans, a new baseball cap, a box of chocolate bars, a large bag of pistachios. On and on, covering the earth with Mark's childhood delights. Irritating. She stops abruptly. Sniffs. Shivers.

Mother, "What's that…that awful odor?" She smells it now. Not a good sign.

You bluff it away, pointing, "The caretaker. Mowing the lawn. Fresh grass. Fertilizer?"

Mother wavers, "No, no...it's not that. Different. Strange. I ...I can't explain. Oh well, never mind. It's gone now. My imagination?"

Your family moves closer beside her. Bradly, Helena, and your father.

Mother whispers, "Now our moment of silent prayer." Eyes tearing, she bows her head.

Your siblings follow suit. You turn away in disgust.

Prayer over, mother perks up, "Let's join hands, and sing."

You walk away as they sing "Happy Birthday" to your dead twin brother. Painful to your ears.

Song over, Mother, cheerfully, "Ok, back to the house for a fine birthday celebration dinner. Roast beef and Yorkshire pudding."

You, grimace, "I hate that pudding shit."

Mother, "It was Mark's favorite."

You sneer, "Twins. It's my birthday too."

The family Mercedes stops in front of your country home, atop a mountain. Two-hundred- foot drop, fenced off by a massive, five-foot stone wall. On the sprawling lawn is a tent, beneath it you see the elegantly set table. Fine China, Tiffany crystal, handmade silver. The family maid serves dinner. Places a soup bowl before your sister.

She winces, "What is this?"

Maid, "Sweet pea, ma'am."

"Smells foul." She pushes it away.

You realize she smells it too. Bad, bad sign. You blow it off, sniff your soup. You lie, "Smells fine to me. At least you made something I like." You slurp it down.

Father, nose in the air, "I smell something foul too."

You, thinking, 'Damn. Now him. Things are going south.' Strange but you enjoy their discomfort.

You, aloud, "When the hell do I get my presents?"

Mother, "Oh, well. Such an impatient boy. I was going to wait until after dinner." She signals the maid, who takes a present from behind the minibar, hands it to you. You tear it open. A framed picture of you and Mark, little boys. Mark dressed as a cowboy, you resentful being his Indian sidekick. Always second place.

You, "This is my stupid present? A picture of him and me?"

Mother chirps, "Mark loved those cowboy games. You always had so much fun together."

You stand abruptly, knock over your chair. You wave the picture in disgust. "Are you going to start the loving-brother bullshit again. Crap on this."

You smash the picture against the table shattering the glass. Your face reddens, rage rising,

"You always change the truth. Mark was a bully. He made fun of me, called me asshead. Do you remember that? He was your precious favorite. I was invisible. Like I'd never been born. You only saw him. Well, you see me now. All these years nobody talked about what really happened."

Father, "That's not true, Michael. It was a horrible accident. You twisted it in your mind. The psychiatrists, the medicine, the therapists helped you see *reality*."

You, "That's what you say. For once try to say it while looking me in the eye. Your big lie."

Mother, flustered, "Be…be nice, Michael. Let's not ruin his day."

"His day! Be nice! You buried the truth when you buried your beloved son. But I'm still here. I am the truth. You want to keep your secret, keep it." You swing wildly, colliding with the maid holding a silver tray full of strawberry parfaits, splattering them across the table.

Mother, loses it, "Oh dear. A fine mess you made of Mark's dessert. You've such a clumsy little boy."

You, "Little boy! I'm twenty-one today. Just like Mark. I'm a man, not a damned little boy." You stomp into the house.

41

Mother calls after you, "Michael, you come right back here and apologize. You're ruining his birthday party."

She starts crying, shaking. Your father goes, comforts her, gives her a pill. "Now, now dear. It will be fine. Michael will calm down and contritely come back to the table like always."

You go to your room. Slam the door. The room you shared with him. You flop on the bed, ruminate. Images crash through your mind. Your mother telling of Mark's easy birth, slipping into the world, no crying, giggles of joy. Then you come out. Always second place.

Mark's endless taunting. Assface. Shit for brains. Stupido. Fool. Shamed again, again, again. Mark scores another victory. From the grave. Your family takes it all as a cute spectacle, which angers you all the more. That time you were so enraged you grabbed him. Threw him to the ground, raised your arm, fist clinched tight, to smash it into his face…your face stares up at you.

"Go ahead assface. Do it, you ball-less coward."

You can't. You lower your arm. You stand up. Run away. Mark sits up laughing.

Your father sends you for anger management therapy. You're inflamed. Nothing changes. It can't. It won't. Your horror film continues, nearing the end. The reality of that fatal day ten years ago. Another birthday party. The twins' eleventh year. The family giggling at the boys playing, but not playful. Mark, yelling. Taunting, teasing, belittling. You, too crazed to yell back. The chase. Mark too fast for you to catch. He clambers up on top of the wall. You follow, you face off, hopping back and forth, air fencing. Mark's verbal sword, his clever retorts. Michael, swordless.

Mark, "What now assface?"

You move closer. Mark backs up, missteps. Down on one knee. Enough time. You reach him as he tries to regain his footing. The 'what now' comes furiously. You lunge out, grabbing, then…heaving Mark over the wall. Your family

42

screams as they run to the wall watching this catastrophe. Mark's body, falling, flailing, helpless, screaming, growing smaller, smaller, smaller. Smashing into the jagged rocks two hundred feet below. Bloody jig saw pieces.

The family buries the truth with a lie. Accidental death.

You snap back to now. You hear your family toasting Mark. It echoes in your head. Enough! Enough! Enough! You walk outside, face, beet red. You hold a 12-gauge, sawed-off pump shotgun. Their laughing stops. Faces fill with fear.

Father, "What in God's name is that?"

You, "A birthday present to myself. The lie stops here. I murdered my twin brother. I'm glad he's dead. I don't have to hear his mocking. No more assface, jackass, idiot, clown. You want to keep your secret ok. I'll let you keep it…forever."

You pull back the pump with a loud ratchet. Aim at your mother.

"At least I learned my manners, Mommy. Ladies first." *Blam!* The shot blows off her head. She sits, headless, against the back of her chair.

"Lady number two, little sister." *Blam! Blam!* Two blasts into her stomach cut her in half. Her torso flops to the ground.

"Now you, dear daddy." *Blam! Blam!* The shots split his chest open, blasts him backwards to the ground, still sitting in his chair.

Bradley, on all fours, scurries to get away. You jump up on a chair. He crawls, not fast enough.

You snarl, "Now, you, big brother. You were supposed to stand up for me. Never there when I needed you."

Michael ratchets the shotgun. *Blam!* The shot crunches between his shoulder blades, splaying him face down on the cold terra cotta tile.

You, smiling, "All gone. But one. The secret dies with me!"

You put hot gun barrel in your mouth. *Ratchet! Click!* Nothing. Frantically. *Ratchet! Click! Ratchet! Click!* Empty. You howl like the beast you've become. Throw the empty gun to the ground, jump off the chair, hit the ground running, time slows as you approach the scene of the crime. The stone wall. You grope to the top.

A sinister smile appears on your face, you scan the massacre, scream at the top of your lungs. "We will all meet in hell, where we belong."

You leap into the void, falling, falling, falling. The odor returns. You breathe it as you cascade. A fetid mélange of decay. The smell of death. *Miasma that you created.*

M

The King & I

Already noon. Been playing and playing my corner since nine. Nothing. My *Foo Fighters* cap at my feet…empty…not a cent. Scorching sun. I'd cut off my jeans if they wasn't my only pair. I smell the city's summer perfume, garbage fumes blended with melting asphalt. Gasp.

I play every song I know. Twice. All five of them. Sidewalk crowds race by. Blue Tooth ears, cell-slapped heads. Eye contact, none. Like I'm not even here. I slam into *Mountain's* Nantucket Sleighride. People grimace, flee. Smart-ass college kids laugh, not with me…at me. Guess it's time to pack it in. I hear a voice. Somehow familiar.

Voice, "Ya oughta be shamed a yo'self boy. Giving rock and roll a bad name."

I turn to see an Elvis impersonator. Head to toe Vegas, white sequined suit, guitar, the whole schtick.

Me, pissed, "Find some other corner, asshole. This one's mine."

He points to my empty cap. "And you're cleaning up ain't cha?"

Me, more pissed, "Screw you, you *wannabe*. Beat it."

He moves closer, leans in, the voice whispers, "You need me, pal."

I push him away. OMG, my hand goes right through him. He steps back, people walk through him. "What tha hell? Gotta cut out the magic mushrooms. I'm hallucinating."

Voice, "You ain't hallucinatin' nothin'. It's me, *The King*. Why they put you and me together, I ain't got no idear."

Me, "You're…you're dead."

The King, "That's a fact. Graceland's a sad, empty palace. Draws a big crowd though."

Me, cold sweat, "A ghost?"

The King, "Uh huh. New breed, *Astral Presence*, whatever."

Me, "You can't be a ghost. I don't see through you. You look solid."

The King, "New software, *Astral 202* or something. Make us more…user friendly, whatever."

Me, "Nobody sees you but me?"

The King, "Lord above saw your act and…wept. Sent me ta straighten ya out. First thing right off…gotta change your friggin' name. Dweezel Crumb? Sounds like something you sweep off the floor."

Me, "You know my name?"

The King, "I know everything there is ta know about you. Your mom, Zappa freak. Dweezel…Moon Unit. Weird then…weird now. From now on you're…" He looks around. Stops at Lincoln Center. "Lincoln, American hero." Looks again…harder. "Broadway, Broadway, broad… broad… Brad… Brad Lincoln. Now on, you're Brad Lincoln. Pack it in, Brad. We gotta lotta work ta do."

The King plucks the E string on his guitar. *Twang!* Magic. We're in my pad.

The King, "This dump smells like a sewer. One, two three…six cats. Six boxes full of poop. Cool dudes don't got no cats…a dog…big one."

Twang! Cats, boxes, gone. Dog at my feet.

The King, "Name's Hound."

Me, "A hound dog…really?"

The King, "Number one on the charts two years. Still covered."

The King scans Brad's living room, "Festerin' pizza, Chinese takeout boxes. Is that yellow thing a couch?"

"I found it in a dumpster."

He peers in the bathroom, holds his nose, "Turds still floating in yer terlet, gag a maggot."

The King plucks the E...*Twang!* Clothes, clean, hung in the closet. Filthy sink dishes clean, stacked, toilet flushes. My grungy apartment, now way Graceland chic.

The King, "Better, but you...you stink."

Twang! Me naked in the shower. *Twang!* Me, in front of a full-length mirror. Coifed, Morrison locks, way tight black leather pants, white silk pirate shirt, black leather boots, red Stratocaster.

Me, "This...this can't be..."

The King, "Sure is, but let's bag the ax. Not your style." *Twang!* Guitar gone. "Dweezel Crumb, meet Brad Lincoln."

I'm stunned

The King, "Now our pipes."

Me, "Pipes?"

The King, "Your singin' voice, compadre."

Me, "I...I sing ok."

The King, "Ok ain't squat." *Twang!*

A huge opera diva bellows at me, "Now you, boy! Now you! From the diaphragm."

Me, lamely, "La, la, la, la, la, la, lah."

Diva, "AGAIN!!! With GUSTO!!!"

I droop. "I...I......"

Diva flails and wails, "USELESS! USELESS!"

The King tucks a Benjamin in her ample cleavage. "Thanks, Hun, I'll take it from here."

Diva fades.

The King, "Guess we need some *heavenly* help."

TWANG! An angelic chorale flutters on high, harps and all, LAAAAAAAAH!!!! All of a sudden, I'm *glowing* like a beacon, filled with light.

Beatitudenously I blast out, "Whole Lotta Shakin Goin On."

Me to myself, 'Whoa Momma squared! Is that me? It is.'

The King, grooving, "Now we talkin, baby, now we talkin'."

The King, deep in thought, rubs chin, "Needs something else. Jerry Lee's got his Grrrrowl, Morrison, primal scream…this new guy upstairs, Kurt something…sounds like shakin' gravel in a bucket, way too loud, but peeps loves it."

I accidently step on Hound Dog's tail. He howls.

The King, "That's it! Right on! The Lincoln Howl."

Twang! Outside. Full moon. Me and Hound howling like crazy.

The King, "Nailed it, baby, posalutely nailed it. Now yer *moves.*"

Me, "Moves?"

The King, "Ya know, struttin ya stuff on stage. Your trademark. I got my hips." Gyrates infamously, "Didn't call me 'Elvis the Pelvis' for nothin'. Waist up only…on Sullivan. Now you… show *me* whatcha got."

I freeze.

The King, "MOVE YOUR ASS, BOY!!! SHAKE SOMETHIN!!!"

I…I do my best. A nerdy twist, trip over Hound Dog. Hound Yelps!

The King frowns, turns to Hound Dog, "Sic 'im' tiger! Sic 'im!"

Hound Dog attacks! Bares teeth, fierce grow. Grrrrr!!!!!

I freak, jump, twist and twirl in the air…twice! I land on my feet, face front, arm thrust in the air, commanding. It feels right.

The King, "You got it, dude…the friggin Brad Lincoln Twist and Twirl! Now you ready for prime time."

Twang! I'm standing stage front at Radium. Packed.

The King, "Take it Brad. You be the front man for *No Exit.*"

Me, to myself, 'No Exit! Hottest players in town. Way cool. Fender bass player, lead, rhythm guitars, maniac drummer, flinging hair-sweat. My dream band.'

Me, Brad Lincoln, twirling. I howl, twist, twirl, twirl twist. Land on my feet, punctuate with arm thrust. Crowd is on their feet.

Wild applause, whistling, cheers, screaming "Encore! Encore!" I'm on fire. I step up to the mike.

The King pulls me back. "No time to dawdle. Got ground to cover."

The King, me, and *No Exit* hit every club in the city. I kill it. I am Brad Lincoln.

The King, self-satisfied, winks at me, his protégé.

Twang! Me and The King, back seat limo. The King holds an album, sexy picture of me on the cover. Me…me!

The King, pearly whites gleaming, "Vinyl, baby, Vinyl, comin' back, big time. Your label, Capital. Top a tha heap. Moved five million, gold, goin' platinum. Next stop, Madison Square, then…*World Tour.*"

TWANG!

OMG! I'm fronting a *mega band*, two drummers, horns, lady backup singers, facing thousands of fans, hot, young girls. Delirious.

The King, "Take a bow Rock Star. They luv ya. Now your *World Tour.*"

The crowd mobs the stage!

The King, "Run for it, Bradley, they'll eatcha alive. Been there done that. Go, boy, go. I'll be waiting outside."

The King vanishes. I flee to escape the groupies. I bust outside. See The King leaning against a stretch limo, smiling. I start across the street. I spot The King, *terror* in his eyes. What the hell? He frantically holds out his palm to stop.

Slam! Splat! Squash! Crackle! Crunch! My own tour bus mows me down. Chicks scream in horror. Weak twang. I stand beside The King. I stare incredulously. An EMT Ambulance screeches up. Painful blaring siren scares the shit outta me. I instinctively grab The King. My arms don't pass through him. I'm shocked.

Me to The King, "You're...you're solid."

An old lady with a Chihuahua in a baby stroller wheels right through me.

Me, "What?" I look deep into the Kings eyes, "You don't mean..."

The King, "I...I do mean. The guy upstairs was hitting on a hot angel. Not paying attention."

Me, "I'm...I'm...I'm..."

The King shrugs, "...as a doornail. Win some lose some. Go with the flow. But I hear you're a big hit upstairs."

We stroll down street. The King's arm round my shoulder.

The King, "Don't fret, kid. I got big plans. Me, you, Jimi, Janis, Morrison...Kurt. A *Golden Gate Concert* set for..."

The King's rattles on, as we walk the stairway to Rock and Roll heaven.

M

Cereal Killer

Angie Porter balances three over-stuffed grocery bags as she struggles with her kitchen door keys. She muses, *'I don't know how mom does it, two jobs, putting me through law school. I can't wait until she gets home from Grandma's.'*

Angie gets the door open, but before she can set down bags, eleven-year-old brother Howie rushes her.

Howie, "Did ja get my AstroCrisps? Huh, huh, did ja get em?"

Angie, "Gimme a chance to…"

Howie, overexcited, can't wait. Attacks one of the bags, pulls out a family-sized box of AstroCrisps. Ducks into his hideout between the washer and dryer. Rips box open with gleeful anticipation. Hand deep in the box, crisps flying everywhere. Nothing. Digs deeper. No prize pack.

Howie, disappointed, "There's no Astro Multiverse Communicator Ring, just this piece of crappy jewelry."

He holds up silver weave chain necklace. A rectangular steel-blue pendant dangles.

Howie, "What a friggin' gyp."

Middle brother Robie, twenty, total hunk, slumps into kitchen, wiping sleep from his eyes. Six two, blue eyes to die for, girl magnet.

Angie, "Well, good afternoon, bro."

Robbie, "Any coffee left?"

Angie, "Old pot on the stove. Nuke it."

Robie pours a cup. Can't wait. Downs it cold. Another. Downs that. Shivers.

Angie, "Easy, speed freak."

Robie, "Late night. Double shift at the bar. Other 'tenders out sick." He eyes the necklace in Howie's hand, "What's that, squirt?"

Howie, "Piece a junk jewelry in my AstroCrisp box."

Robie takes the necklace from Howie, holds it up. "Cool. Can I have?"

Howie, "Take it. You owe me."

Robie, "Deal."

Howie, "Pay up this time."

Robie, "Definitely." He struts out of the kitchen, twirling the necklace around his finger.

Angie, "Oh, plan change. Mom's staying at Grandma's through Labor Day. Have to cancel the beach party."

Howie frowns, "Bummer."

Angie, "We'll be fine. We can do a movie and burgers at Gameworld."

Howie, fist thrust, "Yes!"

Night, Robie's room. He primps in front of full-length mirror, centers the new necklace pendant on his chest.

Robie, "Nice."

He turns to leave. Can't. Frozen. Pendant glows red hot. Scorches his chest. Can't remove it. Power surge streams from the pendant. Flattens Robie against the wall. Jagged lightning bolt strikes the floor. Flames shoot to the ceiling. Electrical storm cloud fills the room. A form takes shape in the cloud. Steps out. Tall reptilian being. Scaly, hairless head, yellow eyes, slit pupils, no nose, air holes, protruding sharp-toothed jaws, long arms, five-fingered hands. Almost humanoid. Split tongue slithers out. Sharp hiss.

Robie, speechless.

Creature steps up close. Face to face. Hisses, oozes into Robie's body. For a nanosecond, Robie's eyes, yellow green slits, split tongue slithers out his lips, other-worldly possessed. Then… back to normal-almost. Robie's body shimmers as he walks out of his room, inhabited.

Robie ends his shift at bar, Nevermind. Band hammers it out on the stage. Robie spots two girls at a cocktail table. Strolls over.

Robie, "Hey Sheila, Marcy, what's shakin?"

Sheila, "Robie baby. Been a while."

Robie, "Way too long. Wanna make up for lost time?"

He discretely dangles a two-gram vial of blow in his right hand, another in his left. They stroll off to his boss Brant's' office. Inside office. Robie, Shelia and Marcy snort the blow off Brant's desk. He pulls them close. Moves, lady to lady, passionate, deep kisses. Nano-moment. Split tongue slithers. Quickly slides down Marcy's throat. She's too high to notice.

Robie's smile seduces, "Hop up on the desk, ladies."

Sheila, "Here? Boss's office?"

Robie nods, reptile eyes. Girls obey, mesmerized. Sheila first. Robie unzips. Straddles. Enters. Finished. Ditto Marcy. He backs off. Hisses gruffly, "I am finished. Go."

Girls shaken by his abrupt manner.

Sheila, "You ok, Robie?"

Robie, "Go! Now!"

His eyes morph reptile. Girls hypnotized, glide out of the office. A beat, then Robie drifts out into the club.

The Porter kitchen. Morning. Angie, and Howie making blueberry flap jacks.

Angie, "Robie's favorite. See if you can get him to come down. He's been sleeping all morning."

Howie, "He does too much of everything." He clumps upstairs. Knocks on Robie's bedroom door.

Howie, "Hey Bro. Breakfast."

A growl rattles the door. Howie instinctively quick steps back.

Howie calls, "Blueberry flap jacks."

Door creeps open. Robie, disheveled, red eyed. "Sorry, Howl, late night. Too tired to eat. Sleepin' in."

Howie shrugs, closed door, traipsed back to kitchen.

Angie, "What's up with the guy?"

Howie, "Too wasted to eat."

Angie sighs. Shakes head.

Hours after midnight, Robie rises, still dressed in his leathers. Ventures across the tracks to the bad side of town. Run down tenements, cracked sidewalks, trashed needles, used condoms, hooded drug dealers, strung out junkies at every corner. Not a cop in sight.

Robie saunters up to a trio of hookers. Redheaded black woman, ultra-short shorts, mesh stockings, platforms.

Redhead, the talker, "You want something sweet white boy?"

Bleach blond, skimpy red skirt, purple panties, spiked heels. "We got somethin' you want?"

Rasta braids, cutoff jeans, orange high-laced boots, *"Ménage a trois* sugar?"

Robie flashes thick wad of cash.

Redhead, "Well all right. Speaks our language. Follow my ass."

They walk to a dark green door. Knock three times. Peep window flips opens.

Redhead, "Freddy, customer. Need a room."

Door opens, trio enters, Robbie follows. Eyes turn to yellow green slits.

The room. Collage of nude bodies sensuously interweave on a large bed. Groping, kissing, raw sex. Women impregnated. Robie stops coldly. Pulls away. Stands. Dresses.

Red, groggy, "Hey, dude. You be forgetting something." Robie, oblivious. Red untangles from her sisters, strolls over, "This ain't freebie night, white boy. Show me that big wad a cash you flashed. You play, you pay. Don't wanna hafta call the management."

Robie, no attention, starts toward door. Red rushes, grabs him by shoulder. He backhands her hard across the head. She drops. Blondie and Blackie spring up, pounce like wet cats. Robie flips them off, a coupla Raggedy Anns. They slam into the furniture.

Door opens. Freddie stands with an old baseball bat, "What the hell's goin' down in here?"

Red, comin' around. "He's trying to stiff us."

Freddy, "That ain't the way we roll, kiddo." Waves the bat. "You wanna leave with yo' head in one piece?"

Robie, groans, grabs his gut, double up in pain. Creature completely morphs out. Robie stands erect. Motionless. Freddy, beyond freaked, swings the bat at the creature.

Creature grabs mid swish, flips, catches handle. One inhuman swing whacks Freddy's head, rips off his neck. A gush of blood spouts to the ceiling. Freddy's head airborne for a millisecond as creature slithers out it's slimy, tacky tongue, wraps it around Freddy's spinning head, slurps it back to gaping jaws. Freddy's face peeks out between creature's clenched teeth, eyes bulging as creature feasts on brains. Crunch! Gulp! Gone! Hookers, blood raining down from ceiling, scream bloody murder! Race stark naked, out of the room.

Beast morphs back to Robie, who casually lopes down steps, out to the street sliding into the night.

Angie, next morning, wakes up. Sees Robie in bed beside her, naked. Freaks. Jumps up. Kicks him.

Angie, "Wake up asshole. What the hell are you doing in my bed?"

Robbie, groggy, "What? Where am ...?"

Angie, enraged, "My bedroom, my bed!"

Robie, "I...I don't know how I got here. Came home late. Musta come in by mistake."

Angie standing, sheet covering her naked body, "A real, real big mistake!"

Robie, "Nothing happened. I swear. I...I never..."

Angie, shouting, "I'm your friggin' sister. Get the hell outta here, creep. If you ever put one toe in this room..."

Robie backing out, "Yeah, sure, never, ever."

Angie, "Mom will throw you out on the street."

Robie, "Please, please. I beg you. Don't tell Mom. Nothing happened."

Angie, "Too late. Your days in this house are over. Get the hell out!"

Robie, "I didn't do anything. I swear." He turns, retreats to his room.

Angie, incensed, slams her door. Sits on her bed, shakes, tries to compose herself. Bursts into tears of rage. Later, checks Robie's bedroom. He's gone.

Later, late, late night. Robie takes refuge behind the bar at Nevermind, disheveled, bleary eyed.

Club owner, Brant Gerber ambles up. "You looked played out Rob."

Robie, "Yeah. Those double shifts."

Brant, "Wanna split. I'll cover."

Robie, "Nah. I'm ok."

Brant, "Least take a break. Stretch on my office couch."

Robie, "That'd be good. Thanks, Brant."

Brant, "I'll get cha when the crowd hits."

Robie walks toward Brant's office.

Later. Club filled to bursting. Brant opens his office door, Brant, "Hey, Rob, need you at the..."

Robie's screwing Brant's wife, Lana, on the desk.

Brant, "What the hell?"

Robie slowly stands.

Lana runs to Brant, pleading, lying, "He roofied me. I swear."

Brant, "Your nose is covered with blow." Back hands her, hard. Lana down. Out cold.

Robie doubles over in pain, creature emerging, jaw thrusts out, carnivorous teeth glisten, black mane becomes scaled brow. Tongue slithers. Harsh hiss. The creature, fully formed, strides over to Brant.

Brant, scared shitless, pulls out a gun, fires. Blam! Blam! Blam! No blood. No harm. Big foul. Brant, traumatized, "What in God's...?"

Lunge! Scrunch! Brant's brain gushes out of his head. Bloody grey matter drips from creature's jaws. Two chews, one swallow, forked tongue licks lips.

Creature morphs back to Robie. He drifts out of the office. Back heels door shut.

Angie in Robie's bedroom, furiously throws his clothes out the window. She gasps. Winces painfully. Grabs her stomach. Reaches under her skirt. Horrified, she pulls back cupped hands overflowing with slimy mass, tiny spheres of squirming life forms.

Crazed, she rushes to bathroom. Kicks door open, stumbles in, flushes mass down the toilet. She vomits, retches until there is nothing but dry heaves. Wiping her mouth with toilet tissue, she turns to see a horrid image submerged in the bathtub. A scale-covered, knife-toothed reptilian raptor, like Jurassic Park. It springs upright, dripping slime. It's eyes flash open. Hideous yellow green slits blaze directly at Angie. Split tongue lashes out. Unearthly hiss.

Angie creeps back as creature's face morphs into Robie's, his eyes swollen, face ashen, gaunt.

Robie screams, "Angie! Angie! It's me. The creature's inside me, Run! Get outta the house." Robie morphs back to monster.

Angie, panic stricken, stumbles out. Mad rush into Robie's bedroom, closes and locks door, shoves bureau against it. Backs into corner. SMASH! CRACK! Creature blasts through door as if Styrofoam and flips bureau across the room like doll house furniture. Angie hides behind bureau. Spots Robie's golf bag. Pulls out driver. Grips it, white knuckled, both hands. Swings. Slams creature's head. Doesn't flinch. Creature morphs to Robie, "Angie! Why are you still here? It's from another dimension. The necklace, a doorway, a portal. Here to inhabit earth. Make women breeders, men...food. The eggs you flushed. They live in water." Robie transforms back to creature, ready to pounce.

Howie, walks into room munching AstroCrisps. "What's all the...?" Sees creature, "Holy shit!" He impulsively throws cereal box at the beast. Direct hit into its gaping mouth. Creature spits, coughs, chokes, gasps. Distracted, releases Robie.

Robie screams, "The window! The window! Shove it out the window!"

They triple-team, slam into the beast, knock it backward, off balance. Creature crashes through the window. Trio looks out. Creature splayed out on the driveway. Robie rips off necklace, throws it out the window. As it falls, a white beam blasts out of the pendant, engulfs the creature. It shimmers, half in, half out of the portal. Explodes to smithereens, entrails flying.

Howie and Robie cheer. Howie, "Definitely the first monster killed by a box of cereal."

No cheering from Angie. She stands, silently, grim face.

Robie, "We won Angie. What's wrong?"

Angie, face contorted, two words, *"The eggs."*

M

Bagged

With
Gita Enders

I met him in Thompson Square Park. Back in the nineties. I'm twenty-five now. I walk home from work, take a shortcut through the park. Even though it was a sunny day, passing the ancient Masonic Cemetery is way creepy. Grotesque gargoyles perched atop weathered monuments like they could jump down on you. Looks like hell. Smells like death.

Someone behind me calls, barely audible. "Excuse me, but you dropped one of your books."

He's tall, way thin, way cute. Snares me instantly. Alabaster complexion, shoulder length jet black hair, dreamy faraway look in those light blue eyes. A silver ID bracelet jingles as he walks. I can't remember how we started talking. He's carrying an armload of books, asks if I want a stick of gum. Wrigley's Peppermint Green pack. I take it.

Me, "Thanks."

Way cute says he's in school, studying at Touro College. To be a lawyer.

I tell him I'm working for a ratings agency at the time. Standard and Poor's or Moody's, doesn't really matter. Just moved out of a nice loft situation in Tribeca. A ground-floor, street-facing, slumlord studio in Alphabet City. Smelled like a rat had died in the wall. No fighting the landlord on that one. He's giving the loft to his dad. Only legal way to lose a rent-stabilized sitch is to make way for a family member.

Way cute asks me if I do heroin.

Me, lying, "Sure."

Way cute asks if I want some now. I think, why not? Another one of my bad ideas.

Way cute guy takes two small glassine envelopes from his crumpled brown lunch bag. His stash. Spills a glassine on the back of his hand, gives me a rolled-up hundred-dollar bill.

I take two quick snorts. My face goes all scratchy. Dreamy, I rub it. Think, yeah, this is great. We continue strolling, talk about nothing. I stop short. Dizzy. Nauseous.

I say, "Hold up a minute." Run over to a corner trash can, throw my guts up. Again...again. Nothing left but bitter bile. Wow! That's heroin. Now, I feel invulnerable. Things look way different. Time slows.

He asks to come over to my place.

I say sure, why not. No bell goes off...again. Another one of my bad ideas.

We do a one-eighty. Stroll back to my place. I open the bed and we screw the snot out of each other for a while. Lazily I lose interest, flip on the tube in the cool dark quiet. Way cute guy says he has to go out, get something. I fold up the bed. He takes his crumpled paper bag, shoves it under the corner of the futon, says he'll be back. I wonder if there's more dope in his bag, but I don't really care. I have the rest of the glassine he slipped me. I do the whole bag. No vomit this time. Just a delirious high. Where am I? Oh, yeah. My place. I have to pee bad. On the back of the john I see his ID bracelet. Pocket it. Gotta remember to give it to him.

After an hour, still way high, 'curiosity killed the blah, blah, blah'. I have to see what's left in his bag. I take it from under the corner of the futon, sit down. Way too heavy to be a stash of dope. I open it. Two metal plates about the size of a dollar bill fall into my lap. I pick one up. It has the image of a hundred-dollar bill etched into it. The other plate, the back of the c-note. Oh my god! Money printing plates. What the hell is this guy into? What have I gotten into? Yet another one of my bad ideas.

I quickly stuff the plates back into the bag...too late. He rushes back in through the door without even knocking. He sits. Nervous. Fills me in. Says he's undercover FBI. Infiltrating a drug cartel. Posing as a heroin dealer. The FBI knows the cartel is moving into printing counterfeit. Needs evidence to shut them down.

I'm still doped. Not sure I'm hearing what he's saying. He rattles on. The cartel knows he's got the plates. Cartel is hot after him...for the plates...and...for his *head*. He's got to make it back to FBI headquarters in DC but he's flat broke. Asks how much I have. Groggy, I check my secret stash. Five hundred dollars. He says we can take a train to Washington.

We? We? Why we?

He says it gives him the cover of a couple. Easier to fool the killers. Says, "Don't bother packing, we're on the run. We go now."

I'm freaked, smacked out. On the run? Wait. Stop. But I don't stop. I keep following. Logic? Well, we fucked. Friends with benefits? Something. I have to help him. Another one of my bad ideas.

Way cute guy, "You gotta coat I can wear?"

I grab my father's old army jacket. Toss it. He puts it on. I fly into my windbreaker, follow him out the door. He hails a cab to Penn Station, constantly looking over his shoulder. Freaks me out more. We get to the station, wade through the crowd. He scans the overhead train schedule. One leaves for DC in fifteen minutes. He pulls me down the step to the track ramp.

Cute guy says, "We'll buy tickets on the train."

Halfway down, he looks back, frightened, whispers, "Shit, it's them. The guys up top in black hoodies. One white guy, one black. Cartel hit men."

He pulls me down the steps, hard. Shoves the crowd aside, cussing and swearing.

We get to the platform. Train running late. He low growls, "Damn, damn, damn."

We weave through the platform crowd. BLAM! A gun shot. Crowd screams. People duck for cover. The two cartel hoodies race toward us.

Way cute pulls us behind a tiled pillar, "You want to live? Stay put."

He takes a gun from his pocket. He has a gun? I want to throw up...again. He glances around the corner. BLAM! Another shot blows a chip off the column. He fires back. Chaos. Crowd scrambles up the steps. Hoodies close in. Cute guy leans out, raises gun to shoot. BLAM! Too late. He's hit in the shoulder, spins around, drops gun. Blood runs down his jacket sleeve.

Cute guy screams, "The gun, the gun, get the damn gun!"

Bravery? Never had it. Survival? Yes. I crawl over, grab the gun. Hoodies, ten feet away. Fight or flight. I don't know how or why, no diff now. Nowhere to go. Fight! Kneeling, hold the gun in both hands, I aim, trembling...shoot. BLAM! Hit white hoodie in the chest. Goes down.

My way cute FBI guy takes off...without me. I'm shocked. He jumps down onto the tracks, running for his life. BLAM! BLAM! Doesn't make it. Two shots In the back. Down. Dead.

Enraged black hoodie faces me. Eyes say everything. Hisses, "Drop the gun, drop it now or you're over with."

Enraged reaches inside hoodie, pulls out a black leather billfold. flips it open screams, "FBI agent! I said, drop the gun now!"

The rest, slow motion, words draw out. Eerie. "Don't make me shoot, girlie. Put it down!"

My hand, auto-pilot, opens. Gun hits the concrete platform.

Enraged barks, "Stand up. Turn around."

Weird. I'm calm now. Slow motion. I turn. He cuffs me. Two uniformed cops, two men in black suits, black ties, surround me.

Enraged, "You're up shits creek, girlie. You just killed an FBI agent."

I yell, "You shot one too, asshole. The guy running away is FBI."

Him, "What guy?"

Me, "He jumped the tracks, ran into the tunnel. He's undercover FBI."

Black hoodie, "Show you his creds?"

Stupid me. I never asked his name. Can't remember what he looked like. So stoned.

Enraged, hood down, shakes his head. "All I saw was you holding a gun. We tracked you down the escalator. Fired shots. Cornered you. Only smart thing you did was drop your weapon, or you'd be a stiff on a gurney to the morgue."

Me, definite, "He comes to my apartment. Brings a bag of counterfeiting plates, says he's undercover to bust a big cartel. I just go along for the ride. I believed him."

Cop, "Nice fairy tale, sweetheart. All I know is I saw you shoot an FBI agent, dead."

Me, crazed. I hyperventilate. "No. What I said. It's all true. The tunnel. The tunnel. He's there. You killed your own man."

Cop, "Fantasyland. You're stoned outta your gourd. I know a junkie when I see one. Musta near OD'd getting high enough to kill a federal agent. You're gonna burn, girlie, burn."

Enraged agent, "You two officers, jump down there, check it out. Careful of the third rail."

Two uniformed cops, resentful, not graceful, slide over the platform, edge onto the tracks. Cautious, they creep along the track, avoiding the third rail. Disappear into the tunnel.

FBI agent yells, "Anything?"

Cops voice echoes, "Nothing. No. Wait. Hey, Cooper shine your light over here. I see something."

Silence. Agent, alert, waits. Cop yells, hoarse, "Better call the coroner. Rotting human remains wedged against the wall. My guess, dead six months or so. A dumb ass accident or third rail suicide."

I break free, still cuffed, jump down onto the tracks run into the tunnel. Only light, cop's flashlight beam quivers over the guy.

Me, "It's him, see, I told you. Wearing the same clothes. Lent him my father's old army jacket. He's still wearing it! Long black hair. It's him! *I met him in Thompson Square Park.*"

Tunnel cop, "Nothing but skull and bones here lady, and what's left of his hair."

Me, "Yeah hair. Black hair. It's...it's him. And the bag. He's holding the bag. The counterfeit money things. Plates, whatever. In the bag."

Cop struggles with latex gloves, finally gets them on, removes the crumpled brown bag from corpse's bony fingers. Opens bag. Out flops a rat-gnawed bagel, empty juice bottle, an opened pack of Wrigley's Peppermint Green.

Cop, "Ain't nothing here, girlie. Your little smack dream. All in your junked-up head."

Hysterical, I scream. They drag me up onto the platform. "It him! I know it! Its him! It's him! I met him!" They drag me up onto the platform.

Cop, to FBI guy, "Junky. Still flying. Delirious."

FBI, "Take her away."

Don't remember the trial. Remember the judge, just what he said. "Murder in the first. Life with no parole."

Armitage Prison cell block, 2020. A Social Worker stands with a prison guard, listening to a young woman's deposition, sent to her cellphone. It's dated 1992.

Young women's Last words, "*... in Thompson Square Park.*" End of tape.

An old woman in her cell. Withered, long unkempt hair, peppered and tangled, she sits on the edge of her bed.

Guard, "Been here for thirty-two years. Been this way the whole time from what I hear. Never leaves her cell 'cept to eat, shower. Can barely walk."

Social worker, "Looks like a refuge from a concentration camp."

Guard, "Yeah. Probably going to die here."

Social worker, "Seen enough." They turn, walk away.

Old woman, motionless, then she fingers an i.d. bracelet like rosary beads.

Chants endlessly, "...*I met him in Thompson Square Park.*"

M

BFF

Whoosh! Thwack! A Smith and Wesson stainless steel ten-inch dual-edged, spear-pointed throwing knife slams into a hardwood target. *Bulls eye.*

David Ingram, the target range owner, says to his companion, "You're up, champ."

Whoosh! Thwack! Whoosh! Thwack! Two more knives quiver side by side hugging the first. David shakes his head amazed.

"Damn girl. You scare me. Just like Ol' Robin Hood splitting his daddy's arrow."

Amy Libert, five ten, short red hair, pixie style, wearing ripped, camouflage cargo pants, a Billie Eilish tee, unbuttoned frayed flannel shirt, and way-scuffed black Doc Martins. Dawg, her German Shepard, raised from a pup, lays coolly by Amy's side.

Amy grins. "Nice try, Davey, maybe next time."

David, "Yeah sure when pigs fly." He walks up to the bullseye, takes a cell photo. "This is one for history books, double whammy. Ever miss your bow, Amy? I mean two-time American Archery champion. Must still have a spot in your heart."

Amy, "Well, been there, yada yada. Knives, double duty. Target range and self-defense. Gang violence's creeping uptown. With my blades I can protect myself…"

David finishes, "… if any dumb ass creep dares cross your path. It's archery without the bow and arrow. Arm, eye, blade."

A silver BMW M3 pulls into the parking area. Doctor Jon Ingram gets out, a tall, delicately featured handsome man with an unkempt shock of dirty blond hair. Amy runs to Jon, jumps in his arms, legs around his waist, plants a huge wet kiss, jumps down. David and Jon, brotherly man hug.

David, "How are things in the ER, Bro?"

Jon, "Too many gunshot wounds. Banger wars. Kids killing kids. Have nothing, get nothing. Tragic." Changes the grim subject, smiling with his arm around Amy. "So, how'd my girl do?"

David, "Simply awesome. I had to document it." Takes out his cell, shows Jon pix of his knife straddled by Amy's doubles. Amy hugs David, planting a big cheek kiss.

Amy, "Couldn't a done it without my Zen master."

Jon, "Gotta move, Babe. Late for our dinner date with your folks. Mommy does not like tardiness."

Amy, picks up her knapsack, walks arm and arm with Jon, a knife still in hand. Parting shot. Arm jerk, thrust. Whoosh! Thwack. Knocks all three knives out of the bullseye. Winks goodbye to David, gets in Jon's Beamer. They squeal off to her Brooklyn Heights cottage. The big rent for such a tiny house was more than she could afford, but she was happy to leave Manhattan's din, hoping quiet would help her finish her new novel. Knife throwing helped her relax and her longtime love affair with Jon didn't hurt either.

Amy and Jon, back home from family dinner, fondling, caressing, kissing, only one thing on their minds, as they move into Amy's bedroom. Slow, caressing, undressing each other. Passion builds. Amy lays across her big brass bed. Jon slides over her. Her arms move around and across his back, fingers entwine, pulling him into her. Face to face, eyes wide open, taking each other in with adoration as they taste each other with tender kisses. In her moment of intense ecstasy, Amy reaches behind her, grasping back bars of her bed, arching into Jon with full ardor. He responds. Their simultaneous orgasms subside. Amy releases her grip on the brass rungs. They sigh deeply, hug tighter, as their post-coital bliss is crassly interrupted by the rasping ring of Jon's cell.

Amy, "At least they let us finish."

Jon smiles, pecks on her lips, answers cell, "Yeah, be there ASAP."

Turns to Amy's blissful grin, softly replies, "You were magnificent."

Amy, "Ditto squared, my love."

Jon dresses, never taking his eyes off Amy's nude body curled up on the bed.

Amy, sleepy, "See you whenever, Doc. Save lives."

Jon, "I'll call when I can m'lady. The image of you lying there will carry me through the night."

Blows a kiss. Down the stairs. Door opens. Closes. Gone.

Amy pulls the sheet up over her, smiles. Falls asleep in seconds. Not for long. Dawg scratches at the door. Her eyes creep open.

Amy, "Ok, Dawggie, ok. Be right there."

She gets up, reaches for the door. Barely creeks open. Dawg rushes in, jumps up, pushes her back on the bed, slurpy face licks.

Amy, "Ok, Dawg, go get your leash. Go on. Go."

Dawg dashes out. Amy pulls on jeans and tee. Slips into her Merrell clogs. Meets Dawg at front door, leash in his mouth. Dawg's tail power wags. They dash out for Dawg's night run.

On the street. Dark. A cool mist curls up from the rain-damp street. It further dims as the single streetlight flickers its way out. Dawg signals Amy with a soft, muffled bark as he spots a figure with his keen eyes. Two shapes come into focus as they glide under the flickering light. A young woman, wearing sweats, a "Fight Hate" tee shirt, and silver high-top running shoes. Her black hair pulled back in a ponytail, she's walking her slick black Doberman Pinscher. The foursome draws close, stops at a fair distance. One never knows with dogs. The Doberman heels automatically. Still as a sphynx. Dawg lopes over to black dog's nose, sniffs around. Doberman does not move a muscle.

Woman's sultry voice, "Rage doesn't make friends fast. Has to psych 'em out." She holds out her hand. "Donnah Farrell. Call me Donn."

"Amy Strong."

They shake.

Amy, "Dawg, meet Rage."

Donn, "Dog? Just…dog?"

Amy, "D-a-w-g. Dawg. Yeah, that's what he is, my dog. Rage is an unusual name."

Donn, "He's earned it. Saved my ass many times. Up for a beer? There's a dog-friendly place nearby."

Amy, "Yeah, Hound Haven. Sure. Love to."

Donn, "I'm buying."

Amy, "First round only."

They smile, take off. Neon sign, Hound Haven. A bar with folks and dogs seated around a huge stone fireplace. The new friends toast.

Amy, "What's your line of work?"

Donn, "Ph.D. candidate, art history. Docent internship at the Gugg. You?"

Amy, "Novelist. Women's biographies. Niche genre. Nothing published."

Donn smiling, "Yet."

Amy, "I like that. Yet."

Donn, "Keep on keepin' on."

Amy's house. Next night. She and Jon finish pasta primavera, Jon's version. Over-cooked pasta, microwaved frozen veggies, supermarket red sauce, Kraft grated cheese. Amy's learned to almost like it, talks with mouth full.

Amy, "Donn's an artist. Giving me New York museums tour. Lunch at high end bistros. Always pays. Very cool."

Jon, "I was wondering what whisked you away."

Amy, "Jealous?"

Jon, "Always."

They kiss. She pulls him toward the bedroom.

Jon frowns. "Not tonight gorgeous. Surgeon on duty. Place is mobbed. Weekend gunshot wounds. Gang wars maxed."

Amy, "Well, at least you had time to make your specialty dish. They are fortunate to have you, Doctor Jon."

They kiss, he splits.

Amy at the Guggenheim, "You must love working here, Donn."

Donn, "Art's my life. I want to get back to painting but gotta pay the rent."

Amy, "Don't I know that."

Donn, "What you got on for tonight girl? Messin' with the good Doctor Jon?"

Amy, "Unfortunately he's on duty till whenever."

Donn, "Then come with me, honey."

Donn pulls Amy to the street. Cab ride.

Donn, "Music's in the air. My go to club. Discord. Trust me. Got a band you must hear. Wrecking Crew Deux., New York's take on the original, legendary LA Crew. City's top studio session musicians playing covers. Delicious."

A beefy guy in a well-worn "Clash" tee opens the glass door. Musical din slams the girls. Full body blow.

Donn yells over the song. "Got us a table up close. Let's ram through."

Donn grabs Amy's hand and drags her in. Amy's overwhelmed at this vast industrial space, packed to the walls. Fans crowd in, dance wildly to Wrecking Crew Deux, wrecking into Hendrix. Donn dances, gyrates, sensuous. Amy, taken aback by the wild scene, is soon overcome by the musical vibe and ebullient crowd. She caves, melting into her own groove. Donn snatches her hand, pulls her close.

Donn, "It's our night, sister."

The two dance, back to back, butts touching, twisting, then turn face to face, real close, lips a micron away. Donn's topaz blue eyes blaze. They dance hard. Sweat streams down their faces. A joint appears, gets passed around. Donn takes a deep drag. Gently touches Amy lips. A signal to open up. Amy shakes no. Donn persists. Amy gives in, lets Donn blow the potent smoke into her mouth, Amy inhales the sweet, strong cloud.

Later at their table, totally wasted on weed and champagne, they babble nonsensical girl gab.

Amy scans her cell. "Way past my bedtime."

Donn, "Hookin' up with Jonny?"

Amy, "Hope so."

Amy and Donn weave through the crowd, out the door. A torrent of cold, driving rain pounds the pavement. A cloud burst. They dash giggling into the street, hail a cab but a young man in front of them gets one first. He sees the dripping girls, opens the cab door and bows, gesturing for them to enter.

Donn smiling broadly, whispers to Amy, "Should we take him on?"

Amy, "I'll pass. Got one waiting."

Donn, "Another time perhaps." Turns to guy, "Thanks so much. Who says chivalry is dead."

Guy, "My pleasure."

They jump in the next cab, dripping wet, laughing, snuggling. Donn pulls a bottle of ice-cold Crystal champagne from her backpack, with two flutes. Pops! Pours.

Donn raises her flute, toasts ebulliently. "To my new *BFF*."

Amy, "*BFF* it is. Let's document our moment."

Amy raises her cell. Donn turns away, but not before Amy shoots. Captures.

Amy, smiling, "Bit blurry but cute. Let's take another."

Donn, not smiling, "No. I don't like the way I look in selfies. I'd prefer you trashed it."

Amy, "Too late. Already sent it to Jon."

Donn, curtly, "I wish you hadn't. I haven't even met him."

Strange silence fills the ride home.

Next day. Jon and Amy in the hospital cafeteria.

Jon, "You girls been spending a lot of time together."

Amy, "I like her a lot. She's smart. Art scene's another world. Learning lots." Strikes humorous classy pose, upper-class voice, "Broadening my cultural horizons. A new me."

Jon, "I'm fine with the old model. How's the novel?"

Amy, "Not good. Been blocked. Hoping Donn's breath of fresh air might break it. I want you meet her, to like her. She's good for me. Just like you are." Peck on the lips. "How bout I have you both over for dinner Monday?"

Jon, "Only if you make your mom's paella."

Amy high fives. "Done deal."

Dinner night. Amy's doorbell. She answers. Sees Jon, Donna and Rage.

Amy, "Well, I guess you guys already met. Come on in."

Dawg runs to Jon, jumps up, licking his face.

Jon, "I didn't forget you, Dawggie." Jon takes a big Milk Bone biscuit from his pocket. Dawg grabs an end in his mouth.

Jon sees Rage, "Well, Dawg, it's share and share alike." Breaks bone in half, offers to Rage. Ignores it.

Donn, "Rage only eats red meat. Fresh."

Dinner goes well. Conversation sparkles. Jon is enchanted with Donn. He gets the expected emergency call from ER.

Jon, "You'll have to excuse me ladies. Duty calls." Jon to Donn, "Great meeting you, Donn. Sorry I gotta run."

Donn, "Occupational hazard. You are excused, Doctor Jon."

Jon whispers to Amy at front door. "I'll take you new *BFFs* out on the town next time. She's smart, cute and those topaz eyes."

Amy, "To die for."

Jon, "You got that right." Quick good night kiss.

Amy cleaning up dinner dishes. A quick rinse, into the dishwasher. Donn walks over to Amy, puts a joint up to her lips.

Amy, "Dishes yes, music maybe, but no pot. I gotta get some writing done later."

Donn, "Just one hit *BFF*."

Amy, "Gonna pass."

Donn takes a big drag. Blows it in Amy's face. "A little contact high for the scullery maid."

Amy finishes the dishes. Plops onto the couch. Donn rushes into the kitchen. Comes back with both arms behind her back.

Donn, "Tatah!" She produces a bottle of Louis Crystal and two flutes. "The drink of our country. *BFF!*"

Amy, "I'm kind of beat. Well, maybe…" *POP!*

Donn, "Too late." Expertly pours two flutes, hands one to Amy. Snuggles down beside her. "To *BFFs*. Nothing can come between us…ever."

Amy, "What's that mean?"

Donn, "It means this." She moves in fast and kisses Amy full on the lips.

Amy jerks away, "Donn…I'm…I'm not into that."

Donn leans in again. "You'll get to love it….and me."

Amy jumps up! "This is getting too weird. I…I think we'd better call it a night."

Donn, "Me thinks I should stay and play."

Amy, "You should leave, please. Now."

Donn stands, vicious, incensed. "So you can slobber all over your doctor boy. You know those ass holes only want pussy. They get tired of the same hole, then split. Always leave when they need new one."

Amy, freaked, "That's *crazy* talk. Please go."

Donn, topaz eyes wild, fierce. "Calling me *crazy?* I'll show you *crazy*, you fucking *cunt.*"

She smashes her champagne glass on the wall. Dawg's on his feet at the ready. Donn looks at Rage. Snaps fingers. His back arches. Teeth bared. Fierce growl.

Donn, "And this is his friendly mode. Wanna see the puppies go at it?"

Amy, "Just get the hell out! Now."

Donn, "I know when I'm not wanted... for the moment."

She snaps her fingers again. Rage calms. Donn walks to the door, opens it, starts out, killer eyes burning on Amy.

Donn, "See ya later, *BFF.* Remember, *best friends forever*, means *forever.*" Slowly closes the door.

Amy freaks, rushes to the door, locks it. Hyperventilating, she leans against the door, catches her breath. Dawg at her side.

Amy, "It's ok boy."

She slumps down on the couch, confused. Tears run down her cheeks. Dawg lopes up, head in her lap. Amy grabs her cell. Autodials Jon, gets his voice message, *"This is Doctor Jon Ingram. Please leave a message at the beep."*

Amy shaking, tears streaming, "Jon, please answer." Amy, hysterical, "I need you. I need you now. Donn's out of her mind. She came on to me. Kissed me. I think she wanted to have sex. Please call. Please."

Amy's cell rings, "Oh, Jon, I..."

Cell, *"Not your doctor boy, BFF. Little ole me. We can chat or I can come over and..."* Amy hangs up. Cell rings, she answers, *"You'll never get rid me. Best friends for life. Unless one of us..."*

Amy hangs up. Cell rings. She lets it ring and ring. A text buzz. She opens. It's from Jon. He can't come...can't leave. Has two vital surgeries. Asks if she wants him to call the police.

Amy types back, "What can they do? She's gone. They'll think I'm nuts. Come as soon as you can. Please!"

Early morning. Amy's place, Jon still in blood-stained scrubs. Amy. Trembling, paces, reaches out for Jon.

83

Amy, "Jon, I...I don't know a damned thing about her. Where she lives, her cell number. I called. Gives me a recording. 'No such listing.' And that's not the half, of it. I checked with the Guggenheim. They never heard of Donnah Farrell. They never had a Docent internship. Lies. She's a total lie."

Jon, "David has a good friend at the police department. He can help. You want to come with me?"

Amy, "I'll be ok. Need to shower her off me."

Jon hugs tightly. Kisses, "Just don't answer your cell. Whatever you do, do not open the door...for anybody but me."

He leaves. She locks and chains the door.

Amy and Dawg in shower. She's lathering him up lovingly. Harsh screech as the shower curtain whisked aside. Donn and Rage.

Donn, "Hi there, *BFF*. Squeaky clean yet? Let me wash your back."

Before Amy can react, P*ffffitt!* Donn shoots her with a tranquilizer dart. Amy grabs the curtain. *Snap! Snap! Snap!* Pulls curtain hooks off the rail as she sinks to bottom of the tub. Donn reloads dart gun, aims at growling Dawg, "I gotta special one for you puppy. Bye, Bye." *Pffffitt!* Dart in Dawg's neck. Quivers. Convulses. Drops...dead. Donn smiles, "Dog food."

Donn throws naked, unconscious Amy over her shoulder. Flops her on brass bed. Binds her hands and feet, spread eagled, to the bed rungs with thin nylon rope, triple wrapped, expert sailor's knots. Tapes Amy's mouth with heavy-duty packing tape. Two layers. Amy starts to come around, Donn and Rage at foot of the bed. Donn pulls a gleaming butcher knife from her backpack.

Donn, "Well now *BFF*. Looks like I have you all to myself."

Meanwhile, at Police Department, Jon sits with his friend, Detective Dan Garrett. Jon takes out his cell. Pulls up the blurred selfie of Amy and Donn.

Detective Garrett, "I'll sharpen it up. Run it. See if we get a match." Mug shots flip by.

Jon points. "That's her. That's Donnah Farrell."

Detective Garret, "Whoa, Momma! Donnah Farrell, aka Carla Hiltner. Rap sheet to Mars. *The Whore Slasher.* Dismembered a slew of hookers. Thought it was some crazy John out for revenge. Street hookers figured out who the butcher really was. Not a man...a woman...one of their own. All the dead girls were Carla Hiltner's girl lovers who dumped her. You know her as Donnah Farrell. Cops found Hiltner in the dead girl's apartment, sitting yoga style, catatonic, in front of body parts. Her black Doberman feasting on girl's entrails. Hiltner didn't even put up a fight. Officers cuffed her and escorted her out."

Det. Garrett continues, "Pinscher followed 'em out. When the Officers opened the front door Hiltner screamed, 'Rage, now!' Dog took off, speed of light. Never was seen or caught. Hiltner-Farrell was doing a life sentence at New York Psychiatric hospital for the criminally insane on Wards Island."

Jon, "Was?"

Det. Garrett, "Escaped. Two years ago. Shivved a guard. Disappeared into the ether. She's on the FBI's most-wanted list."

Jon, "Well, she's reappeared with her insane dog. She's started a friendship with my fiancé, Amy. Amy's all alone. These monsters are after her."

Det. Garrett, "Your wife needs protection. We need to move. Don't have time to bring in the FBI. I'll call for back up, alert the Feds on the way. Ride with me. Let's go."

Back at Amy's cottage, a blast of hot sun burns through the bedroom window backlighting Donn. In partial silhouette she looks like an angel from hell. Strips. Flings her panties and bra onto Amy's nude body, picks up butcher knife, starts to climb up on Amy. She hears sirens as police cars squeal up.

Donn, nonchalant, "Sounds like we have company."

Jon and Garrett enter Amy's house. Jon calls out "Amy, Amy…"

Nothing. They see Rage eating Dawg's eviscerated corpse. Garrett takes out his gun.

Amy gagged and tied, hears the living room noise. Uses her well-muscled throwing arm to pull brass rail lose. Slips rope off. One arm free.

Rage sees Jon, bares teeth, deep growl, races toward him. Vaults couch, teeth gnashing. *Blam! Blam! Blam!* Garrett blasts Rage, midair. Dog's momentum carries it. *Caarash!* Rage plunges through the front window, wooden frame and glass flying. Jon and Garret run to the window, look out. Rage, vanished.

Garrett, "What the hell? I hit that damned dog three…"

He never finishes. A gleaming butcher knife curls around Garrett's neck. *Slisshhh!* Donn slits his throat. She runs to Jon. He tries to push her knife arm away. She knees him in the groin. He buckles. Starts up. Donn buries the knife deep in his shoulder. He falls to his knees. Donn holds knife with both hands. Raises it high to stab Jon in the head.

Amy's voice, "Hey BFF, flash those killer blues my way."

Donn's head snaps to face Amy, standing nude in bedroom doorway.

Donn evil grin, "Come to join my party?"

Amy, "Even brought presents." *Whoosh! Thwack! Whoosh! Thwack!* Two gleaming S&W knives slice into Donn's topaz blues, protrude out the back of her head. Bloody eye slime drips down her shocked face.

Amy, "Like I said BFF, *Eyes to die for.*"

Donn head snaps. Stares inhumanly at Amy, whispering harshly, "BFF means forever, baby. Forever." Then crumbles lifelessly to the floor.

Months later, Amy, Jon, David at the target range.

David, "You look happy with a bow back in your hands."

Amy, "Feels right. Those Smith & Wesson blades found their bullseyes."

David, "Ok kid, let's see if you still got your chops. Beat this." Raises his bow and arrow. *Thwang! Whoosh! Thup!* Bullseye. Dead center.

Amy holds her custom Hoyt Formula XI Recurve Olympic bow in one hand, yanks a red bandana from her jeans pocket, wipes sweat beads from her brow. Drops bandana. Slips a lethal triple-razor arrow from her quiver. Removes sheath.

David raises his eyebrow. "What the hell are you doing with a Wasp Sharpshooter Razor Point? We're not deer hunting."

Amy, wry smile.

A breeze blows up. She instinctively calculates how the wind velocity will affect her shaft's trajectory. She lifts her bow, aiming a bit off kilter, takes a deep breath. Let's her shaft fly. *Thwang! Whoosh! Scrack!*

David's eyes go wide.

Jon's jaw drops, "I'll be damned."

Amy's shot split David's arrow in two. His shaft's ribbons curl alongside her arrow.

David, "Well. I do believe Robinhood deserves a prize. Be right back."

David walks into his office, returns carrying a big, wobbly box. Sets at Amy's feet. "Go ahead, open it." She pulls back the flaps. A boisterous German Shepard puppy jumps into her arms. Tears of joy run down Amy's cheeks as she cuddles her puppy. Jon and David, Amy's two favorite men, watch gleefully as Amy hoists her puppy high in the air, proudly dubbing him, "Dawg!" A true BFF.

Shish! Swish! Swish! Thuck! Thuck! Thuck!

Three razor point arrows, with supernatural speed and accuracy slam through Amy, Jon and David's necks, severing their spinal cords. They drop instantly. A figure dressed in a black hood, holding a hunting bow, stands twenty feet behind the bodies. The puppy wobbles to Amy's body. Sniffs, licks, bites her calf, drawing blood. Licks it ravenously.

The hooded figure calls sharply "Rage! No!"

The puppy freezes. Turns. Faces the figure and slowly morphs into an adult black Doberman Pinscher.

Second call, "Rage! Come! Heel!"

The dog runs to the black-hooded figure. Stops statuesque by its side. The bow vanishes from the figure's hand. The specter, black dog, fade into the mist.

BFF? Not this time. Try again.

M

Darkroom

A high fashion photographer's life, not as glamorous you'd think. Myriads of too-beautiful models…they all start to look the same. Numbing. Just another job. Then *WHAM!* No…not the models…the models' agent, Samantha Brooks, CEO, The Brooks Agency. Way cool, way calm, way collected. Class on the half shell. Venus. Lauren Bacall at thirty-five. Shoulder-length, page boy coiffed hair, dirty blonde, oversized blue tinted glasses, tailored Cassini silk business suit, Italian high-heeled shoes, a solid gold Tiffany ankle bracelet. Knocks me out. Unapproachable. I don't even try. I just keep shooting. Prada's spring line. But I can dream.

In the darkroom, printing the day's shoot. Can't trust anyone else to do it. Burn out assistants by the dozen. Alone. Deeply immersed. Outside my cave, universal redlight sign, DO NOT DISTURB.

A knock at the door. What dimwit can't see the damned light. Pissed, I walk through the black security curtains, close the darkroom door, step into the small antecroom. I unlock, open the door to the front desk. There. Samantha Brooks, leaning against the jam.

Samantha, "Loved what I saw on the monitor. Guess that's why you cost so much. Got anything to show me?"

Before I could recognize the innuendo, Samantha pushes me inside the anteroom, kicks the front door shut with her heel, pins me to the wall.

Samantha, in a sultry voice, "This door lock? Oh, here it is." CLICK.

Dare I say it? Outrageous. Yes, she is. With me. Two hours later, adjusting her clothes, she saunters into the studio. Not even turning asks, "Dinner? Per Se? Masa? Your call. Tables at both."

Me, to Samantha, "Absolutely." To myself, 'My, my, oh my.'

The affair continues for months. I expect it. Desire grabs my libido, twists it, twists it again. I'm addicted to a woman I know little about, save she owns the hottest modeling agency in the city, country, world. Captivated. Falling. Hard. Was she using me? Of course. For what? I don't give a damn. She had me, all of me. I'll pay the price.

Obsessed. I need to know more. One evening, late, late, dead of winter, coldest ever, we leave my Soho loft, always at my place, never hers...a whole brownstone, flat iron district. I escort her to her limo. She grabs my hair. Deep kiss. Icy breath.

"Goodnight. Tomorrow."

"Of course."

"Till then."

Limo peels. A peeling limo? Puhleeze. Cut me some slack.

I decide to tail her home one night. Wanna see her infamous New York City digs. I follow her in my Porsche. Her limo drives to a desolate, rundown part of the city. This ain't no Flat Iron District. I park a block behind, get out, follow her. She walks purposefully through side streets and alleys, block after block, ...then disappears.

I search. No luck. Loud voices from a boarded vacant store. I peek through a window. Mindboggling. Candle lit room. Circle of dark purple robed woman, wearing disfigured masculine face masks. The only differentiation, their shoes. There it is. Gold Tiffany ankle bracelet.

Samantha Brooks, delivers a hissing, bitter rant, "The male patriarchy governing the world must be obliterated. We must infiltrate the belly of the beast, disembowel it from within until…it is dead. Extreme prejudice our mandate."

I turned to slip away. Accosted. Two masked women, robed. One wears white diamond encrusted heels. I spot them on my way to the ground. Something wacked me hard. Unconscious. Inside the room.

I revive, face to mask with the ranting leader, Samantha Brooks, shouting, "Now they send spies to eradicate us. An example must be made!"

I'm stripped nude, bound to a chair. Brooks grabs me by my hair, no kiss this time. Her apostles smear me with lipstick, mascara, eye liner. The group bursts into wild, crazed laughter, pointing at me. Brooks holds a mirror up to my eyes. My face, horrible, bizarre, debauched.

Brooks forces liquor down my throat. Douses me with it. Two women drag my chair out onto the middle of the deserted street. A makeshift sign slapped on my naked chest: "DEAD MAN".

Brooks, sternly. "Enough."

The women scatter in the frigid night. I shiver. I see someone. My savior? A bedraggled homeless man from the shadows. "Whatya been up to buddy? Whatever it was, looks like ya lost," he cackles. "You need some TLC. Got money?"

"As much as you want."

Later, at a police station. I smell of liquor. I'm draped in a blanket. Lawyer by my side. I tell Detective Dalgliesh, yes, Dalgliesh, my ludicrous, terrifying tale. I do not identify Samantha Brooks. She's mine. She'll pay for this.

Monday. My studio. Closing out the shoot, there she stands. Sultry smile. Not a glimmer that I know…everything. I conceive my revenge. Tech nerd buddy, Arch Clafield, fashions a remote control Minox, triggered by a wireless switch in the darkroom. Hide the camera atop the wall timer. The switch, under the enlarger.

I instinctively know the inevitable moment will be manifest...it is. I take her, now reviled, with a perverse sexual vengeance, kissing, pawing, tearing. Nude, sweat-glistened bodies making not love, nothing near it. Making hate. Hit secret switch. Camera silently clicks. It ends quietly. We dress, go to dinner, part with a steamy kiss.

I process, and enlarge every print, making sure Samantha's face is clearly recognizable. I stand, stare as they hang, drying. I slip them into a manila envelope, label it in red marker SAMANTHA BROOKS. I get to the deserted street before the group arrives. The dreaded torture cell. I use my Amex platinum to slip the lock. Stale, high-end perfume redolence. I choke, place the envelope in the center of the room, and leave.

Next day. My entire studio staff, way freaky, nonstop cacophony. Arch, smiling slyly shows me the Daily News front page. Samantha Brook's disfigured frozen body in a drainage ditch, kicked to death. Victim of an unsolved brutal murder. Tucked under her twisted ankle, gold Tiffany bracelet intact...a white diamond studded shoe.

I didn't wish her this. This is what she got. Revenge served *frigid*.

M

Charity

I'm late for a brunch with my attorney. In the middle of a bitter divorce. Took me half an hour to find a safe garage to park my new Mercedes.

Me, I tell the guy, "There's a velour cover in the trunk. Drape the car...gently."

I start away. Greedy guy holds out his hand. Stares me down. I crumple up a ten, toss it across the car roof. He grunts away.

I'm walking the New York minute to my meeting. A voice calls out.

Voice, "That's right. Walk right past me. I'm invisible."

I turn to see an old man in a well-worn wool tweed three-piece suit, sitting on a bench, holding a picket sign, FEED THE HUNGRY, in bright red paint-dripping letters. I take out a twenty, step back, hand it to him. He rips in half, then into confetti, tosses it in the air.

Old man, "I don't want your damned money, Fauntleroy. I want some attention to be paid."

Me, "Hey old man, go to your rally I have business to..."

Old Man, "I am the rally, Mr. Bigbucks. Your kind fawn over droughts in Africa, all those poor starving people. Hell, there are poor starving people right here. Kids living on free school lunch, only meal they get."

Me, blubbering, "I...I give plenty to charities..."

Old man, "Name one."

Me, "I...I can't name them offhand. My accountant handles...for tax write-offs..."

Old Man, "So why waste time jawing with an 'overwith'? My word for the aged, which I am. Ya'll got no more use for us on your capitalist treadmill...*Overwiths*. Go, go little Richey. Don't let an old man's plea get in your way. Have a nice big fancy lunch. Don't forget the wine, white with fish, red with meat. *Bon appetit.*"

Me, Feeling compelled to stay when my cell rings. Roy, my attorney, on speaker phone. Roy's harsh rasp blares. "Bradley, where the hell are you? I've been waiting an hour."

Me, "Ok, Roy, ok. Be there ASAP." I spin to leave.

Me, to old man, "Sorry. Gotta run, Mr. Overwith."

Old man, "So be it. You got biz. Go do it."

There's something about this man. Mesmerizing. He smiles broader.

Old man, "How about buying a useless *Overwith* a cup of coffee? My go to spot's just down the block."

Me, strangely compelled, "Yeah. Sure."

I follow. It turns out to be a rundown old bar.

Old man grins, "Well, coffee isn't my drink of choice. A beer would be nicer." We go inside. I inhale the stagnant air. He holds up two fingers to the bartender.

Old man, "Hey, Billy, go for the foreign brew, my new friend, Bradley is paying."

Old man sticks out his hand. "Hello Bradley. Might as well introduce myself. Doctor Willis P. Higgins. PhD. English lit. Early retirement. They were ready...I wasn't. Benched for the duration."

Me to Dr. Willis, "So you're headed to a rally?"

Dr. Willis, "Like I said before, I *am* the rally. Somebody has to remind the haves about the have nots."

I finish my third beer. A lot for me. Got a good buzz going. Relaxed. Nice. Not my usual anxious self. Dr. Willis goes on about the inhuman treatment of the underclass. I'm listening, hard. What he says pierces my corporate heart. Empathy. A thing I'd lost floats up. My cell rings again. Know it's Roy. I don't answer.

Dr. Willis, "Turn that damn cell thing off." He yells to the bartender, "Hey, Billy." He holds up two fingers, "Two more here."

'Tender nods.

Me, "My bladder calls. Three is way over my limit. I gotta..."

Bartender, "Relieve yourself. The right-hand side of the wall phone. When you go in, feel for the pull string."

Me, I enter the men's room. Pitch black...dank. I weave through the darkness, find the string. Pull it. The room is empty...I mean no stall, no urinal, no sink. No window. Just an empty room with a front and back door. What the hell? I gotta go. Bad. I'll use the woman's room. I rush to the door. It's locked. I'm gonna piss myself. I run, hold it in, painful, gonna burst. Reach the back door. Bust out into a dark alley. Piss in a corner. Ahhhhh. Relief. I hear a shuffle of feet. Look over my shoulder. A ragged young man slips out of the dark. Opens a switch blade. CLICK reverberates. I'm freaked. Nowhere to run, nowhere to hide. Ragged young man approaches, menacing, followed by the rag-tag band of homeless.

Me, shaking, "You...you want money? Here, take my wallet. I don't carry much cash. A couple hundred. Mostly cards."

Dr. Willis pushes his way through the crowd. I'm surprised. Dr. Willis says, "Don't want your money, Bradley." Then calls to the crowd, "Jeremy, the bottle."

Jeremy, a short grimy man, waddles up carefully, holding an old basket-wrapped Chianti bottle. Dr. Willis takes the bottle. Hands it to me.

Dr. Willis, "Drink this, son. Make things easier."

Easier? My arm reaches out. I drink the wine. It's sweet. After the first sip I feel calmer. I drink more. I become limp, crumble to the ground.

The rag-tag people move in close. Drop to their knees. Old woman slips off my Italian loafers.

Me, I bark, "Be careful with those, Italian. Made to order."

I realize how ridiculous this sounds under these bizarre circumstances. Old woman cackles. Takes off my socks. Cackles again. Then, unbelievable, puts my big toe in her rotten-toothed mouth, bites it off. Oh my god. I feel no pain. Then they all dive in. Eating my toes like they were asparagus tips. Kid with switch blade kneels beside me.

I hear Dr. Willis, "Rusty here got laid off from a butcher shop. He's a damn good meat cutter."

Rusty expertly cuts up my pants leg, rips my trousers up to my crotch. Two guys bring out a greasy gas barbecue grill, light it up. Jesus! Rusty filets my calves, my thigh. Still no pan, no blood…just this nightmare from hell. Rusty tosses my thigh filets onto the grill. They sizzle like a steak.

I smell good. Rusty flips the filets over, cuts off a morsel, passes it to the old woman.

Old woman, "Needs salt. Too tough. Not like that flabby rich lady last night."

Rusty slashes open my chest and abdomen. Slithers out my liver. Flops it on the grill.

Old woman, "Grilled liver! My favorite. Great with onions. Anybody lift any onions?"

Stiletto kid, slashes my wrists, drains the blood into a jelly jar. Sips. Frowns. "Tastes flat. Got any that *Wiss Ter Sherie* Sauce?" A bottle's tossed from the back. He shakes on a splash. A young woman plops a wilted celery stalk into the glass.

Dr. Willis grins, "New drink. Bloody Bradley. Pass it around."

They get to my head. Some dude from the back comes forward with a hammer and chisel.

100

Old Woman stops him, "His brain's fer dessert. My favorite, brain puddin'."

I whimper, "Please, stop this insane carnage. I'm being eaten alive! What in the hell's happening?"

Doctor Willis, holds up his placard, wide bloody smile, "Like the sign says, Bradley... *FEED THE HUNGRY!*"

M

Mr. Lucky

Dusk. Light drizzle. Left my hat at work. I'm visiting my mother's grave. Ritual. Her birthday. Louise Weller. Died ten years ago. I'm in a deep funk. Just got fired. Third job this year. School kids called me 'Mr. Lucky' as a joke. I failed seventh grade. Twice. Never graduated. Took GED's. Failed. Never got a diploma. 'Mr. Lucky.'

Open my deli bag, unwrap my tuna sandwich. Shit, it's baloney...I hate baloney. Pissed. Crumble it up throw it back in bag, take out another package, unwrap. A cupcake, hope it's Vanilla, Mom's fav. Shit. Not vanilla. Strawberry. She was allergic to strawberries. Fish my pocket. Take out a birthday candle. Of course...It's broken. Stick in the cupcake anyway. Droops sadly. Take out my disposable lighter Flick! Flick! Flick! Empty. 'Mr. Lucky.'

An old guy in filthy overall holding a rusty shovel comes from behind a tall monument.

Toothless smile, "How's it going, boy?"

"Could be better."

"Ain't it the darn truth."

"You the Caretaker?"

"Sort of. Mind if I sit?"

"Be my guest."

Sits down real, real, slow. Groans, "Ooooh, dear Lord."

"You ok?"

"Muh knees. Bone on bone. Never had time ta get 'em fixed. Rainy days make 'em worse."

I hold out my hand, "My name's Wilbur. Most call me Willy."

"Call me Jesse." He slips off his work glove, holds out his hand. I grasp it.

Damn! His hand comes off. I'm holding an armless bony hand. What the...?

Jesse, "Sorry man. I hate when that happens."

Takes back, tucks hand and glove into his overall front pocket. I'm shaken, to say the least.

Jesse, "My bunions acting up too." Crosses his legs. *Creak! Crack!* Pulls off his work boot foot's still in it. Puts boot and foot in his lap. Unlaces boot. Pulls foot out. Massages it.

I'm freaking out. Gotta cut back on the weed.

Jesse, "Got some friends comin' by. Mind if we join ya? Only come out full moon."

I look up. Big white face in the night sky. A diverse crowd forms zombie-like right out of Michael Jackson's "Thriller."

A woman comes to the front. It's...it's my mother, looking like she did after funeral parlor makeover.

Mom, "Hello Willy. Good to see you, Babyboy."

Jesse, kindly to Mom, "Sit next to your boy, Louise."

He stands. Hops away on one foot. Mom sits.

Mom, "Give us a kiss, Babyboy."

I...I do. A hunk of her cheek comes off in my mouth. Gag. Spit it out. "Pa-tooey."

Mom, "Sorry about that, Babyboy. Mortician's wax. They filled in where your father hit me with his hammer."

"Oh, yeah. Right. Sorry about that, Mom."

Mom, "Stop with the 'Mom'. You and Brian always called me *Mommy-dutsy*. Such cute little boys. Miss chasin' ya outta the kitchen."

She takes a compact from her ragged purse. Looks in the mirror. "Oh, dear me, I didn't have a chance to freshen up." She calls out, "Momma! Momma! Got any lip gloss? Some rouge?"

My grandma, not looking too good either, steps out of the gang to the forefront.

Grandma, "Sure little one." Searches in her torn ShopRite plastic bag. Never used a pocketbook. She hands gloss and rouge to my mom. Mom drops her compact. It rolls away.

Me, "I'll...I'll get it for you...Mommy-dutsy."

Mom, "Don't bother yourself, Willy."

"I'll get it for you...Mommy-dutsy."

Mom, "Really don't need it, Willy." Mom twists off her head. Sets it in her lap, puts on lipstick and rouge.

Head talks from her lap, "That better, Babyboy?"

"Ah, yeah. Sure. Much."

Mom screws her head back on. "So, Willy. What you been up to? Lou Ellen must be a teenager by now. And the twins?"

"Everybody's fine, Mommy..."

"...dutsy."

Me, "Right, Mommy-dutsy."

Mom, "Ever reach your dream, get to be a rock star? You and your brother made so much damned noise practicing with that band in the basement."

Me, "Ah, no. Remember. I got my hand caught in the car door."

"That's right. Brian slammed it. You always had a penchant for bad luck."

Me, "Guess I did." Pull back my sleeve to check the time. No watch. Oh right. Muggers. Got my wallet too.

Me, "Well...Mommy-dutsy. I gotta be going."

I stand, see headlights in the near distance. A hearse, winding up the road. Way too fast. *Bam!* Blows a tire, skids, jumps the curb, heads straight at me. I do a deer in the headlights. Freeze.

"Whoa, Momma, ah, Mommy-dutsy!" *Crash! Splam! Squish!* The impact spreads me all over Mommy-dutsy's tombstone. It gets quiet. Way too quiet. Strange. I stand beside

107

Mommy-dutsy and her pals, all staring at me. Me, squashed against her tombstone.

Mom, "Well, Babyboy, guess bad luck's frowned on you again. Welcome to our club, baby."

Me, "Oh my gosh." I'm a graveyard newbie. Mommy-dutsy hugs what's left of me.

Everybody sings *"Happy death day to you, Happy death day to you, Happy death day dear Willy…"*

I turn and see a new tombstone, mine. Big chip off the corner. Figures.

WILBUR WELLER-1992-2022.

REST IN PIECES.

Last line misspelled. My arm falls off. Forever, 'Mr. Lucky'.

M

Little Black Dress

Paris, France, December 1975

Petite, adorable, vivacious, Avione Manisur. Her long, glistening black hair swishes as she scurries down Rue Montoruril, boutique shopping bag in hand, breathlessly bursting into her parents' shop, *Manisur's Fine Tailoring*. Her mother, Magda smiles, reflecting the young woman's glee.

Avione, flushed, "Momma, Momma, guess what!" She dances around the room. "Forneau Magnus's Christmas gala at his Chateau. He has invited everyone. I need a dress. One that will make them gasp."

Avione's father, Poupau, enters the shop front through living quarter curtains, beams, "The Belle of the Ball, eh, Princess?" She ran to him. A big hug. Kisses both cheeks.

Avione, "I hope so, Papa." Then to her mother, "Will you make me the dress, Momma? Black, short, the Chinese silk I love? Please? A dress to go with these!" She pulls a shiny new pair of black stiletto heels from the bag.

Magda, in shock, "Mother of God...how much?"

Avione, checky, "No matter. My Christmas present to myself."

Poupau asks, "Maybe more sensible shoes?"

Avione, "Pish tosh, Papa. It will be Christmas Eve. My first gala."

A cab pulls up behind a line of black limousines fronting Magnus's Chateau. Majestic. A liveried doorman opens the cab

111

door. Out glides Avione, in her little black dress, stiletto heels, her mother's mink boa. Exquisite. Scintillating.

Monsieur Forneau Magnus, on front steps, greets guests. Spots Avione, scrambles down to her, enraptured, "Avione, Avione. Your mere presence graces my gala."

Avione, flushed, "Thank you, Monsieur Magnus."

Magnus, "Take my hand. I will escort you inside." He places her hand atop his. Avione feels uncomfortable. Magnus, well-known for his lecherous ways, holds her tight, smiling a wide, yellow-toothed grin.

The unlikely pair strolls through massive oaken doors to the ballroom, draped with fresh pine garlands. A mammoth spruce dominates, lights reflecting off gold and silver ornaments. Waiters with trays of champagne and hors d'oeuvres weave through the crowd.

Magnus says, "Avione, you must excuse me for a moment. I must attend to Judge Lounard and his wife. I will keep my eyes on you."

A slight, unseemly pat on her bottom…again. She feels another bit of discomfort. Magnus disappears into the festive throng. Avione is instantly surrounded by office colleagues. Both men and women are wide-eyed at her sight. She dances, dances, dances. A once-in-a-lifetime evening. Her smile never leaves her face.

Magnus appears behind her. "Avione!"

She flitters, blushes, "Oh, Monsieur Magnus. You startled me."

Magnus, oozing charm, "A dance to make an old man happy?"

"Of course, Monsieur Magnus."

"Forneau, please," he says, charmingly.

A deeper flush, "A pleasure…Forneau."

They dance. He holds her a bit too close. His hand slides down way too low as they swirl the perimeter of the gaping crowd. The grandfather clock chimes twelve.

Magnus raises a glass, Avione firmly in hand. "Merry Christmas to all. A ten percent raise in all your stockings."

His employees cheer, toasting back. Magnus finger snaps! Waiter appears.

"A chilled bottle, two flutes, my library, *tout de suite!*"

Magnus, to Avione, "You will join me?"

Avione, apprehensive, "I believe I've had my...."

Magnus, "Nonsense. One more Christmas toast. My library, *plus priv'e, s'il vous plait.*"

Avione, "It's very late...my parents..."

Magnus, "My driver will take you home." He furtively glances left and right. They slip into his library. Close the door. He whispers, "Sit my dear, the red velvet chair. My dear departed wife's favorite."

Avione complies, nervous.

Magnus, "You look regal. A princess."

Avione, "So...so my papa calls..."

Magnus, "Oh? Really? Whatever." Takes a silver foil box, replete with gold ribbon from his top desk drawer, strolls to Avione, holds it to her. "A *cadeau*...a gift."

Avione, "I couldn't, Monsieur Magnus..."

Magnus, "Forneau, Forneau...please."

Avione, stands, slight tremble. "Forneau, your, your raise was more than..."

Magnus, "Just open it. I insist."

Avione unwraps revealing a diamond necklace.

Magnus, "My mother's, my wife's, now yours."

Avione, frightful, near to tears, "No...no...I cannot. I cannot. I must leave. Please, Monsieur...Forneau, please."

Magnus, insistent, "Let me put it around your elegant neck."

Avione backs away.

Relentless, he advances again. Gruffly places the diamond necklace around her neck. Spins her around to face a floor-to-ceiling mirror. He holds her tight, by the shoulders.

113

Magnus, "See, what did I tell you. Now a real princess. Perfect."

Avione tries to break away. Magnus pins her against the wall.

Magnus, "A Christmas kiss...your *cadeau* for me." He moves in.

Avione ducks under his arm. He grabs her, pulls her to him with a yellow-toothed smile. Forces a kiss. His hands groping like an octopus.

Avione jerks away, lipstick smearing. "Stop! Stop! Please."

Magnus in again...stops dead...wild-eyed. Screams, "AAAhhhhhh!!!! God! God! Ahhhh!..."

He weaves backward, releasing Avione. She steps away... revealing her *stiletto heel* buried deep in Magnus's head. Thin blood trickle from the wound, down his face. He slides slowly down the mirror to the floor. Reflected mirror image. Horrifying grim tableau—Magnus... Avione's heel embedded in his skull. She stands paralyzed in disbelief. Magnus's loyal staff breaks through the door.

Avione's trial moves with dispatch. Magnus owned the town. His still-loyal staff testify to the wanton behavior of this brazen hussy who forced herself on this honorable old gentleman. The judge, Monsieur Lounard, along with a bought and paid for jury. All men. The foreman hands the bailiff the verdict.

Bailiff, "To a man, the jury finds the accused, Avione Manisur, guilty of the murder of Forneau Magnus."

Judge Lounard stands pointing at Avione "Penalty, death, execution by *Guillotine.*"

Marseilles Prison. Grey stone, windows barred. Poupau and Magda sit beside Avione on a grimy, bug-infested bed in her airless cell. She gently strokes Magda's teary cheek.

Avione, "My dear ones. I will be fine. I will be with God. One request. I am to be buried in my black dress...please...no discussion."

A loud clatter of metal keys. Two matrons in black uniforms unlock her cell. "It is time. Stand!"

One matron holds her, the other shears Avione's glorious black mane. Magda and Poupau are devastated. A wide-awake nightmare.

Matron commands Avione, "Arms behind! Now!" She aggressively cuffs Avione's wrists, pushes her out the cell door. Magda and Poupau shuffle behind.

Execution courtyard, a stone-cold moonless night. The grim party enters. Gallery, Magnus's family, Magda and Poppau, far side facing a high platform, displaying a monstrous death machine, a sixteen-foot-tall guillotine. Its sharpened steel slanted blade embedded in a massive block of lead.

The two matrons half walk, half carry the suddenly unfocused Avione up the platform steps. Court Executioner, Forsange la Cour, grabs her arm. Three-hundred beheadings, this one no different.

Official calls out, "Avione Manisur, do you have any final words of repentance?"

Avione, defiant, *"Vous condamnez une jeune femme qui s'est veng'ee contre l'agression sexuelle besstiale d'un homme."* You condemn an innocent girl fighting to protect herself against horrid sexual attacks from a beast of a man. Forevermore, these monsters will pay for my unjust sacrifice. Now, as you steal my life, I will wreak my eternal revenge.

La Cour rips Avione's prison smock down over her shoulders, forces her onto the wooden guillotine platform. She instinctively struggles, a small bird in a snare. La Cour lifts her head, pushes her neck into the bottom stock, slams down the top. Avione, no escape. Her tiny hair-cropped head, all that's visible.

La Cour peers down at the court official. Official nods. La Cour releases the blade. *Clank! Swoosh! Slam! Avione's head...*it's here...it's gone. Blood gushes from the oval of her severed neck onto the guillotine blade.

Magda faints. Poupau too frozen to help.

Later at the state morgue, Magda and Poupau hold handkerchiefs to nose. Scant protection from the foul-smelling preparation mortuary. In a far corner, a roughhewn wooden coffin holds the body of their beloved daughter, a blood-stained paper bandage hiding her wound. Magda gently pulls down Avione's hiked-up black dress. The solemn pair wince as each hammer blow confines Avione in this box for eternity.

Magda buries her head in Poupau's chest, "Take me from this place, Poppau. *Maintenant!*"

Magda and Poupau walk back to their shop. Magda's face goes ashen. Her knees buckle. Poppau grabs her, saving her from falling. He sees what she sees.

"This cannot be..."

Avione's black dress hangs in their shop window. Magda uncontrollably rushes in, rips the dress from the hanger. Runs and descends the rickety wooden steps to the dank, dark cellar. She pulls the string, lighting a single hanging bulb. Opens the coal furnace door. Red heat blasts. She winces...then throws Avione's dress onto the flaming coals. Poupau reaches her. They watch the little black dress burn to ashes.

Magda, shaking, "I...I cannot stay in this city any longer. Avione haunts my every thought. We must get away. If we stay, I will die. We must get away. *Maintenant!*"

Houston, Texas 1976, Tavis Street

Rundown neighborhood. Dangerous. A hand-painted sign, *Manisur's Fine Tailoring* swings in the hot wind. Inside, Magda is in front of her new American sewing machine. "You know what today is?"

Poupau sipping coffee at a small table. "A year to the day."

Magda, "We will go to the church, pray and light a candle."

Poupau flips through the curtains to the shop front. He screams in terror, "Magda, Magda! Magda!"

She rushes through the curtains. Drops in a chair. "Dear God in heaven." Avione's little black dress hangs in the shop window. "It has found us."

Two chicly dressed sisters, Ally and Serena MaGraff walk down Tavis Street, huddled close together.

Serena says, "I don't know why I listen to you. Coming to this part of town. Even in the daytime, it gives me the willies."

Ally, insistent, "Hush up, Serena. I was drawn to the ad in the *Houston Local.* Couldn't get it out of my mind. A new French shop, handmade clothes. I need something to wow the hell out of them at the Exchange's New Year's Eve party. Just keep walking, eyes straight ahead. We're almost there."

They stop in front of the tailor shop. "Here we be, *Manisur's Fine Tailoring.*"

Ally spots the little black dress in the window. "Oh, my god. This could be my lucky day. Look at that killer dress." Ally pushes ahead of Serena, rushing into the shop. A little hanging doorbell tinkles...old world.

Serena, "Smells musty."

Ally, "Don't be such a prig." Ally beelines to the black dress in the window. "This is a 'look-at-me' dress for sure. Wonder if it's my size?"

Poupau, parting the backroom curtains, a strange glaze in his eyes. "It was made for another, but I know it will fit perfectly. You look petite, 7 maybe 6."

Ally, "Hello sir. Good eye. Petite six."

Poupau, "But a tiny bit larger, excuse me...bosom...35?"

Ally, "You know your stuff, Sir. 35 and a half. I like to squeeze into a 35."

Poupau, "Yes, yes of course. Low cut...*de rigueur.*"

Serena, "She likes her cleavage to..."

Poppau, "I understand. Please, try it on." Poppau takes the dress slowly off the hanger. Hands it to Ally.

Ally, "Silk?"

Poppau, "Chinese silk. Custom-tailored by my wife. It was returned by the one who designed it. Please, step into the dressing closet."

Ally swishes in, tries the dress on. Bursts out looking incredibly edible. She caresses her curves. Sashays around the three-sided mirror. "No bra, no panties. Fits like my skin. Is this dress sizzlin' or what?"

Poupau, "Like it was made for you."

Ally, "I wonder why any woman in her right mind would ditch such a prize?"

Remembered pain flashes in Poppau's eyes. It passes. He merely shrugs.

Ally, "Oh, well. What's the damage?"

Poppau, *"Pardon moi?"*

Ally, "How much does it cost?'"

Magda quietly enters through the curtains. Stands behind Poupau.

Poupau, ever the salesman, "Well…well, it is Chinese silk…so…"

Magda gives Poupau a slight foot tap, silencing him. "I made it long ago in Paris. It's been hanging here forever."

Ally, "You do incredible work. What are you asking?"

Magda, "For you, my dear…nothing. Our *cadeau* for you."

Ally, "Pardon me?"

Magda, "Free. For you, free. Wearing it will be your payment."

Ally, "Oh, my Lord…I…I can't."

Magda, "Please. An anniversary. You are our first customer on this special day. A *cadeau*, a…a gift."

Poupau, "Our daughter Avione's …"

Another Magda foot tap. She quickly finishes the sentence, "…birthday. She is in Paris." Magda reaches behind the counter, swishes out Avione's black shiny stilettoes. "And these. Also, free. Go with the dress."

118

Ally, breathless, "Oh my. I must give you something." She reaches into her purse.

Magda, "No, please. Our pleasure."

Serena, under her breath, "Take it and run girl."

Ally blanches, "I don't know what to say…". Eyes wide. Unmoving. Then, *"Merci beaucoup pour votre amiable generosite."*

Magda, *"N'ai pas peur. Elle te prot'egera."*

Ally, *"Bonne chance avec votre magasin. Au revoir, Madame et Monsieur."*

Poppau, *"Adieu"*…Under breath…*"Princess."*

Ally snaps back, "Ah, yes. Thank you so much. Definitely my lucky, lucky day."

The sisters exit the shop. girly giggling.

Magda, woodenly, "Lucky…yes…your lucky, lucky day."

Outside the shop. Serena asks, "What in the world was that? You don't speak French."

Ally, quizzically back, "French? What are you talking about? I wished them good luck and goodbye."

Serena, incredulous. "What the hell did she say to you?"

Ally shrugs, speed walks ahead, nonplussed. "She said bless you my child, farewell."

Serena stands gawking, "Bless you?"

Ally parks in her designated spot in The Stock Exchange underground garage. Instinctive frown as she hears a cat whistle, turns to see her boss, Preston Ward. Tipsy. Clearly he's started partying early. Walking to the elevator, a bunch of VPs in tow.

Ward, "Hey, Alley Cat!"

Ally ignores him, not on her A list.

Ward, "Hot dress, sexy shoes. Looks feline ta me. Come on up with us…Ally."

She speeds up, walks ahead, scoots into the elevator, bangs the door-close button. Doors start.

Ward and his boys rush, yelling, "For damn sake Ally, hold the damned…"

Elevator closes. Ward slams his fist on the door. "Little bitch."

The elevator opens to a huge loft, over-decorated. Gross. Ward's style. Ally steps out. Male heads snap like heat-seeking radar, eyeing her *décolletage*, short, skin-tight dress, way high stilettos. They rush up, offering drinks. Ally sees Mark Linkletter, a pal. Waves. Mark, waves back. Hurries over.

Mark to Ally, "You look great! Need help fending off the herd."

Ally, taking Mark's arm, "Always to my rescue."

At the bar. Mark, to the 'tender, "Two frigid Sapphire martinis, no vermouth allowed. One olive. Let it sink."

Ally, appreciative, "You never forget a thing."

Mark, "About certain friends…"

Ally cradles his face. Nails polished black. "…with benefits…"

Way long kiss. Mark, recovering, "My good fortune." Drinks arrive. They lift and toast.

Gruff voice, "Wasn't very nice…Ally." Ward barges into the bar, wedges himself between Ally and Mark. Snaps fingers in the air. Twice. "Hey, 'tender, gimme a double…triple, single malt, best ya got, pronto. And another whatever for the lady. Her boyfriend can fend for himself."

Ward turns to Mark, sneering, "Markster, me and your lady gonna talk private business here. Get scarce."

Ally, to Ward, "Don't be so rude."

Ward, "He can have ya back when I'm done."

Mark to Ally, "It's ok. See you later for a dance." Lip peck. Mark leaves.

Ward, "What da ya see in that guy? Got none of your class. Alley Cat…"

Ally cuts him off, "You call me that again, I'll…"

Ward teases, "Slap my face? I'd like that. Anyway, I got somethin' in my office you might be interested in."

Ally, "Whips and chains?"

Ward, "Ya know...Ally, there's a reason why you flew through the ranks so fast."

Ally, "My 24/7 blood, sweat, and tears paid for that."

Ward, "And you had a guardian angel."

Ally, "Let Me guess."

Ward, "I'm serious...Ally. Five minutes in my office. No likey, you flee."

Ally, dubious, "Just business?"

Ward, "My word of honor."

Ally, wary but curious. Ward picks up her drink, "C'mon. Just business."

Ally, against her better judgment, follows Ward to his office. He opens the door. Hand gestures 'come on in'. Closes the door, walks to his desk, pulls out a sheaf of documents. VP position. Hands papers to Ally to sign.

Ally scans documents, beams. "This is for real...no strings?"

Ward, "No strings. Welcome aboard." Holds out his hand. They shake.

Ally, "I'm stunned, and appreciative. I won't disappoint."

Ward, coy, "Maybe someday your name makes it to the wall beside mine. Ward & MaGraff, nice ring. Join me in a celebratory...toast."

He takes a mirror from his desk drawer, filled with a mound of cocaine, replete with razor blade and ubiquitous, rubber-banded C-note straw. Cuts out four thick lines. Hands it to Ally, "Ladies first."

Ally extends a quick palm down, "I Pass. Not my thing. Now if we're finished with business, I'd like to get back to..."

Ward, "Mark Linkletter? That loser." Snorts two lines, "You and me are a better pair."

Ally, "If this is going where I think, I pass on the VP." She starts to leave. Ward grabs her arm...hard.

Ally, "You're hurting me."

He spins her back for a rough kiss. She slaps his face hard!

Ward, "Like it rough…Ally, huh?" A jolt of extreme misogyny, Ward decks her. She falls back on his desk, semiconscious. He steps close. Looms large.

Ally, "You touch me and I'll…"

Ward covers her mouth roughly. Pins her down with his sheer mass.

Ward, "You'll what, Alley Cat?"

Ally bites his hand. Tastes blood. Ward jerks it from her mouth.

Ward, in pain, "Jesus…Jesus Christ!"

Ally blows a chuck of his bloody hand in his face. Top of her lungs. "HELLLLLP MEEE!! HELP MEEEE!!!"

Ward, mindless with rage, ignores her screams. Ally struggles. Powerless. Ward's knee spreads her legs.

Ward, "I always win this game. Smart ta play along, Alley Cat." His hand creeps up her dress.

Ally sees a desk pen, grabs it. Jabs it full force into his arm. It enrages him more.

Ward, "Damn bitch! You're an animal!"

Mark and two other guys hear Ally's cry, burst through his office door to help. Weird. Their legs freeze in place. Blam! The office door slams shut…by itself. Mark tries to speak. Can't. Ward out of his mind with rage, oblivious to the intruders. Pulls the pen from his arm, moves back…just enough. Ally slides free. Backs away. Ward, dripping blood, lunges. Can't. Feet locked.

Ward, "What the hell?"

Mark and the others can only stare in awe. Speechless. Suddenly, Ally, blank-faced. A statue. No fear. She glides to Ward, faces him. Raises her arm, a stiletto shoe in her hand.

Ward, smirks, "What the hell you gonna do with that, little Alley Cat?"

Ally, in a trance, *"Ne vous approchez pas d'un pas. Tu le fais a tes risqué et pe'rils', sale bete!"*

Ward, "What the hell you talkin', bitch?"

Ally *slams* her shoe heel into his eye, rips it out. Blood spurts from the socket.

He screams, "Ahhhhh!!" Instinctively slaps his hand over his eye wound. Mucous and blood ooze between his fingers. "Jesus Christ you little bitch, I'll..."

Ally raises her arm...again. Then...slams the stiletto heel into the center of Ward's head...leaving it there. She commands, *"Non! Vous ne ferez rien. Tu es déja mort!."* Ward drops like a sack of fat.

Ally, *"J'ai finis...pour le moment."* Turns away. Turns back, *"Je reviendrai jamais."*

Ally blinks, blinks again, shakes her head to clear. Takes in the scene in disbelief. "What? What...?"

Mark, now free, runs to Ally, standing over a dead man, her shoe heel embedded in his blood-soaked head. "You had no choice, Ally. You had to defend yourself."

Street front, Ally's apartment. A police car pulls up. Parks. Officer hops out, opens the back door. Ally jumps out, disheveled, dried blood splatter on her face. She nods to the officer. Nods back. He acknowledges self-defense. Police car departs. She speeds to the entrance and goes inside. Feverish. Steps into elevator, exits on her floor. Bursts into her apartment. Runs to the kitchen. Jerks the dress over her head. Opens utility drawer. Finds poultry shears. Snips the little black dress into shreds. She grabs a long wooden spoon. Jams the black silk fragments, piece by piece, into the protesting garbage disposal...until...it's gone. Ally stands naked, shivering. Lowers her head, hands cover her face. Torrent of tears. Relief. Over.

One year later. To the day. A well-dressed young woman, Sandy Foster, and her friend Lois Freeport hurry along Tavis Street in Houston, Texas, past boarded, vacant tenements.

Lois asks, "Why would anybody in their right mind open a business in this disgusting neighborhood?"

123

Sandy, excited, ignores Lois. "There's the sign we're looking for, *Manisur's Fine Tailoring.*"

She stops short...The little black dress hanging in the front window captivates her.

Sandy squeals, "Oooh my, oh my. Looky that. Hot, hot, hot. Gotta nab that one."

She and Lois dash into the shop. Tingling bell. Sandy's eyes focus on the little black dress. Flits over, feels. Sandy, "Silk?"

Poupau passes through the curtains, "Chinese. Custom-tailored by my wife. It was returned by the one who designed it."

Sandy, "For sale?"

Poppau, "Of course."

Lois, "Well, one gal's mistake is another gal's prize."

Sandy, "Size?"

Magda, from behind Poupau. "Oh, it will fit. Like it was made for you."

Poupau lifts the dress off the hanger, hands it gingerly to Sandy.

Magda, "Oh...and these." She holds up the black stiletto heels. "They go with the dress. *Tenue parfait.* A killer outfit."

M

Favor

The whole damn thing, all seventy-eight years...my life. I'm wiped out. Empty. My wife, the love of my life for forty-eight years died after a long and painful illness. I was her sole caregiver. The world dropped from under me. No children. Friends all passed. Alas, me, alive, alone. The sound of my echo the only voice I ever hear. Had enough. Suicide? Often contemplated. I'm a devout coward. Loathe the slightest pain. So... I'm still here.

Time for my walk, recommended by my primary, by my cardiologist, also my shrink, my therapist, my physical therapist. All with one goal. Keep me...Wilson McAllister, going forever. Forever. The word made me cringe. Forever for what? I'd accomplished whatever goals I had. Most important thing in my life was aiding my wife's peaceful transition to wherever. Wish she'd taken me with her. My future? Screw it. I could give a damn. Never crosses my mind. Smirk inwardly at the ridiculous bucket list my psychiatrist brings up each tele-visit. I have no fear or anxiety about dying. And no bucket list. An atheist. Atheist since conception. Heart stops pumping blood to your brain. Lights out. Fertilizer. Dust. I wish for it every day.

Exit the elevator onto the dark street. The night. A dear friend. It was chilly. I pulled up my topcoat collar, lit a cigarette I was forbidden to smoke. Head to my go-to restaurant for the forbidden double martini dinner. Pass an alley. Two young thugs jump out. One white. One Hispanic. Whitey has a gun, a small black revolver.

Whitey, "Ok, Old Man turn around, hands on the wall."

I comply. So what? No fear here. Death wish granted? "Wallet's in my coat pocket. No cash, just cards, but I tell you what." I turn around. "Do me a favor. I'll make it worth your while."

Whitey, "Cool your jets, Grandpa. You ain't in no position to ask for no favor."

Me, "Hear me out. It's simple. You do the favor, take the credit cards in my wallet, back pocket. Code's on the back of my driver's license. Hit the ATM. Clean me out."

Hispanic, "Listen to the dude, Reg. His cards, the codes. Big time."

Whitey, "Ok, old fart, what's the favor?"

Me "Kill me."

Hispanic, freaked, "Kill you? You nuts man?"

Me, "Empty your Saturday Night Special into my heart. Time it stopped beating anyway."

Whitey, "You're crazy old man. Kill you? We get life."

Me, "Who would know? Bang, bang, you scram. Piece a cake. You two live high on the hog. Ok, lads…the favor." I open my coat. A clear, clean target.

Whitey, sweating bullets, chaotic gun waving. Panic. "You wanna kill ya self. Be my guest."

He throws the gun at me. I catch it. They disappear in the alley, running likes bats out of hell. So, it's up to me. Can I do it?

I look at the gun. Weird. Licorice? A candy gun. I haven't seen one of these since I was a kid. The jokes on me. I laugh. I laugh hard. First time in years. I bite off the barrel and chew. Always loved black licorice. Nostalgia. A warm rush. I laugh, chew and laugh and chew. All the way back home. Content.

Guess the boys did me the biggest favor of all. A moment of joy…and my life.

M

Nitwit

I was a golden boy, tall, blond, good looking, smart as a whip. My parents' only child, their clichéd pride and joy. We were a financially well-off liberal family, my dad a prominent attorney, Mom a college professor. My mom started teaching me to read while still in her womb, telling a story to her belly...to me, every night. Her teaching never stopped. I was reading by myself by four. Never without a book in hand. I'm reading Macbeth, my beloved cat Hamlet curled up on my lap. Ham was part of our family. An equal, not a pet, a family member. I was deep into the play.

I flinched when my cell rang, a blast of Beethoven. I fished my cell from my back pocket, answered. The Chief of Police. Bad news. My parents in a car accident. Both dead. Nauseous, I drop the cell, run to the bathroom. Barely made it. Threw my guts up into the toilet until all I tasted was bitter bile.

My golden life ended. I was forced to live with grandparents, my father's parents, my only living relatives. Being dyed-in-the-wool, far-right Republicans, they had shunned us for years because of our liberal views. We never associated with them.

I was thrown into living hell. I had to call them "Grandmare" and "Grandpere." Ridiculous. They wasted no time going to court to gain control of my trust fund. Until I was twenty-one. Doled it out like misers. Insult to injury, pulled me out of private school.

Grandpere, "Goddamn stupid to flush good money down the john goin' to that ivory tower private school, stuffing your head with commie bullshit. This is America. Public schools are free. You need to rub elbows with the stinking masses. Let 'em knock some sense into your privileged little head."

So, public school it was. I sucked it up. Endured it. Grandmare found fault with everything I did. Said my parents had raised a *nitwit*. Grandmare constantly badgered me. Her catch phrase, "Nitwit, you always do the wrong thing." Sheer torture. My only friends, Hamlet and books.

My grandparents despised Hamlet from day one.

Grandmare, "Damn cat fur everywhere. Clogs the air conditioning filters and my vacuum. All over our clothes. Even found some in the kitchen. Near food. No telling what disease it's carrying."

Grandpere, venting rage at Ham, "Filthy friggin' box a dirt he craps and pisses in. Smells like a damned outhouse."

Then the straw that broke the camel's back. Unknown to me, they put Ham's litter box on the back porch. When he had to go, no box. Sabotage. He relieved himself in the living room. Number one and number two. On their precious Persian rug. Grandpere crazed, grabbed Ham by the scruff of the neck, opened the kitchen door, literally threw him. Threw him out into the yard. Snow on the ground. Ham was so freaked he bolted into the woods.

Grandpere, "Now on, he's an outside cat. Keep it that way, nitwit."

It was agony every time I heard Ham scratching at the door. The noise drove Grandpere mad. One day, no more scratching. Ham disappeared.

Grandpere, "Wild thing ran away. Good riddance."

Me, heartbroken. I mourned for days.

One of my jobs was bringing in wood for the fireplace. Every time I went out, I scanned the wood line, hoping, praying that Hamlet would find his way home. Home? I never wanted to go back inside that hell hole again. Maybe I should run away, too. Not the right thing to do.

I took a long walk in the woods to calm down. Then...I saw it. Ham's body. A boulder had crushed his skull. I knelt beside him. So devastated I couldn't even cry. There it was, a cigar band. Grandpere's brand. Bastard murdered my cat. If I opened my mouth, I...I didn't know what he'd do. Hit me, throw me out of the house? He'd been dying to do that. I could see it in his eyes when *I did the wrong thing*. I held my anger in...again. I was powerless...again.

The next insult, a hunting trip. Hunting was their big thing. Hunting with guns. I hated guns as much as my parents hated them. Avid anti-NRA forever. My grandparents' station wagon, NRA bumper stickers, both sides. They loved to hunt quail and doves. The dove, icon of peace. Who'd want to kill one? Eat one? My grandparents, that's who. It sickened me.

One day Grandpere thought it time for me to become a man and learn to shoot. "OK, Nitwit, time to learn gun safety. Get your lazy ass up and dressed. Going to the range."

I felt ill the first time a 12-gauge shotgun was forced into my arms. Heavy. Lethal. Horrid. Smelling of gun oil, and cordite. I pretended to pay attention. My brain would not let it in.

We began weekly jaunts to the range to shoot clay pigeons out of the sky. My first shot knocked me on my butt. Grandpere laughed his ass off. Didn't even offer a hand up. Thankfully, the ordeal ended. Back home I escaped behind a book, no Ham to caress or be lulled by his purr. But the trauma was not over.

They made plans to use Grandpere's vacation to go hunting. Took me to a big box hunting apparel store, fitted me with the uniform, a bold red and black checked wool winter coat, Wellington rubber boots, a ridiculous hat with ear flaps that matched the coat. I looked like a fool. Even the store mirror laughed at me.

It took forever to drive to their lodge, me holding back my car sickness lest I barf, which I did once. Their wrath always at the ready, they made me clean it up myself with vomit-soaked tissues as Grandmare yelled at me. *I did the wrong thing again.*

We got to the lodge, had a disgusting dinner scooped from cans. Corned beef hash fried in a pool of lard, succotash, white bread, black coffee you could stand a spoon up in. No milk, my favorite drink. Not allowed in their house. A drink for babies. Early bedtime. A good night's rest for the hunt. I had barely fallen asleep when Grandpere shined a blinding light in my face.

"Up and at 'em Nitwit!" he shouted. It was 4 am, dead of night.

Another two-hour drive. Me, carsick, nauseous as usual. Then a three-mile walk down a leaf-strewn path to a dense frost-covered forest…where it happened.

Later. NYC police station, Fluorescent lit room. I'm seated at a table for a video deposition. Police Detective Wilmer is the presiding officer.

Wilmer, "I know this is rough for you. We can stop whenever it gets to be too much. Just look straight at the camera, son. Tell us what happened."

Me, "I…I don't know how to start. I loved them so much. Before they died my Mom and Dad had Granny and Gramps over every Sunday for dinner after church. Dad, Gramps and I played catch till it was time to eat. Granny and Gramps were right there hugging me after Mom and Dad's accident. I turned sixteen this year. They threw me a big party. Gramps gave me my first shotgun so he could teach me how to shoot for the big quail hunt we were planning. Granny had a special quail recipe, my favorite."

Detective Wilmer, "Let's go back to events if this afternoon."

Me, "It's kinda hard to talk about. It happened so fast."

Detective Wilmer, "Just run through what you remember about what actually happened."

Me, "Well, we started out through the woods. I made a terrible mistake, *did the wrong thing*. Accidently left a live round in my gun. Forgot all about it. I was not paying attention to where I was walking. I was really excited about bagging my first quail. I...I tripped over a rock. My gun went off...hitting Granny. I killed her. It was all my fault."

"Grandpa was hysterical, screaming, 'Oh my god what happened?'

I told him. He hugged me tight, 'Don't worry Son,' he said. 'It was an accident. God will forgive you.'

Gramps ran to Granny, lying on the round. He knelt beside her crying. 'Oh my God, my God, how can I live without you Glendine? You are my whole life. Don't worry my dear. I will be with you this very moment'. Then he...he did it. To himself."

Wilmer, "What did your Grampa do?"

Me, "He...he unholstered his side arm, his .44. He put it to his head, pulled the trigger. Collapsed right on top of grandma. I didn't know what to do. Then I took Gramps' cell phone, called you...the police."

"Accidental homicide by misadventure. No crime. No charges. Boy called. Did the right thing."

I often recall how easy it was. The shell, purposely slid into my shotgun. Fake stumbling. A ruse to kneel. Then aim, shoot Grandmare. Took her head off. Grandpere in shock, crouching over her body. I sneak behind, slip his .44 revolver from its holster. Then...oh so slowly... place it against his temple, pull the trigger. *Blam!* Blew his brains out. Wipe my fingerprint off the trigger. Place the .44 in Grandpere's hand. Put his finger on the trigger. A slight press. His print, my freedom.

I got my inheritance. Five million dollars. What to do? Law school, the right thing. Successful practice, the right thing.

Reading on the beach outside my ocean front villa in Maui, with my two cats Mac and Beth snoozing in the shade, *the right thing.*

I finally did all *the right things.* And no one calls me *Nitwit.*

M

G.R.

I just turned 75 and thought, well, this is it, the time when everything falls apart, and it does. I don't walk so well. I run worse. If danger comes my way I'm screwed. Being this is the Big Apple, anything can happen and does. Still, I limp into Central Park every morning. My only aerobics. Keep a keen eye out for the gate ledge, a trip trap for ancients. I work up five drops of sweat and sit on a bench, winded. It's early, 6:30 am. I get out this early to beat the heat. Gonna be 98 by noon. The park is strangely vacant. I stare at the void wishing my knees would stop hurting.

I spot a dark figure, floating very, very slowly toward me. Its full image comes into view. Over six feet tall. Head-to-toe black-hooded robe, a long sickle rests on its shoulder. Uh oh, this does not look good. My health isn't great, but not this bad, I don't think.

The robed figure stands before me, huffing and puffing.

Robed figure says in a deep, reverberating voice, "Mind if I join you, I'm beat? Feet are *killing* me. *Killing me.*"

How apt. I struggle to speak, sounding sincere and extra nice, "Of course, of course, please, please, sit…and rest."

Robed figure sits down, leans its sickle against the bench, and holds out a black-gloved hand. Speaking firmly, the robed figure says, "The name's G.R. I use my initials, cooler."

"Nice to meet you…Gee…Gee, G.R., I'm Mi… Mi… Mick."

"Like in Jagger," he quips. "Almost met him last year."

We shake. His grip, hard, boney.

139

G.R., "Gonna be a scorcher today, already eighty-seven, want a beer?"

"Sure, sure, why not," I quivered.

G.R. reaches his black-gloved hand under his robe, pulls out two ice-cold bottles of beer, flips cap off both of them with a thumb, thrusts one at me.

"Le Chaim," he said wryly, as we raised and clinked bottles. "Beer's loaded with carbs. I'm trying to put on a little weight. I feel like a bag of bones."

He chugged his beer. I followed suit.

"Nothing like a cold one after a hard day's night. Cools me out. My job is very stressful."

"Wha...wha...what do you do?" I ask stupidly.

He ignores me, then says, "Mostly use the old sickle to thin out the dead grasses. Damn things, they never stop growing."

"They?" I questioned cautiously.

"The fields, the lawns, and the old weeds."

Me, "Lawns, weeds, I thought you were the Angel of Deat..."

"Hey," he interrupts me. "Haven't you ever heard of a euphemism?" He continues, "I'm on twenty-four seven, my supervisor's got it in for me. Says my production's too low. I tell him it's modern medic... oops, I mean chemical advances. Fertilizer, my worst enemy, keeps them healthy and strong. Hell, they're living longer and longer, tough to cut down, dulls the sickle. Got to sharpen the damned thing by hand, twice a day, and wipe off the...the...the sap, yeah, the sap. Think he'd give me something more efficient, like a weed whacker."

"So, you could mow the hell out of them!" I said, momentarily maniacal, caught up in this bizarre repartee.

G.R., "I gotta admit some of it's on me as well. I got older. Slowed down."

Me, "I know what you mean. Those old joints wear down."

G.R., "Speaking a joints, want a hit?" He pulls out a dube and lights it, takes a long toke.

Me, "No thanks. Did my share in the sixties. Gotta keep a clear head just to get through the day."

G.R., "Tell me about it. By quitting time I'm burnt to a crisp." He flips out the roach, sighs, and goes on, "Well, duty calls. I should get back to it. My break time is almost over. Maybe see you around again sometime, Mick."

Me, "Ah, sure, yeah."

G.R., "Well, nice jawing with ya, Mick."

Me, "You too." I wish he'd stop saying my name.

G.R. quips, "Later Bro."

Me, praying to self, 'Yeah, much, much, much later.'

He raises his open hand. I respond instinctively, high-fiving.

"Right on!" G.R. laughs.

He moves wearily, drags the sickle upside down behind him. Floats away,

G.R. gets smaller and smaller, until he disappears. I rub my eyes. Is this a dream? A bad bit of cheese? My meds need tweaking? Then I see the two empty beer bottles on the park bench. Reality chills me. I've been chatting with the...the...I can't say the words. G.R. it would stay. How can I explain this without being committed to the psych ward? I get up, grab the empty bottles, toss them into a trash container. I start the long walk back to my apartment, nervous, looking over my shoulder. My pace turns into a gait, then into a jog, then an all-out sprint. Damn, I could still take off when I need to. What am I running from? I don't want to dwell on it. I get to the gate. G.R.'s leaning against the post, sickle resting on his shoulder.

"Just where do you think you're going, Mickster?"

M

Splop

My second visit to a new dermatologist, Dr. Joan Wolfram. First visit, the doctor found a suspicious spot on my arm, possible basal cell carcinoma. She snipped a piece for biopsy.

Doctor, "I'll call you with the results."

She calls. "Sorry to report the biopsy results are positive. You need to have surgery."

Me, "I've had a few spots removed. I know the drill." Receptionist schedules my procedure..

So, here I am in her operating cubby getting prepped. Dr. Wolfram enters the room wearing light green surgical scrubs.

Doctor, "You just need a local for this. I'll spray the area with some lidocaine. Just lie down."

I do as she says. The spray is cold.

Doctor, "I'm beginning now."

I wait. Impassive.

She says intensely, "Halfway. Almost there. Hold on. Got it. Done. Not so bad, was it?"

Couple beats of quiet.

Doctor Wolfram, disturbed, "Whoa. This…this is weird."

"Meaning…?" I inquire.

Doctor, "It seems to…to be…oh my god."

"What is it, Doctor?"

I hear a strange *sploping* sound, then…muffled gasps. I sit up quickly, see the gaping incision in my arm. I stand abruptly, turn to face the doctor. She's sitting on the floor, back against the wall, covered with blood. The blood-drenched chunk of

145

my skin expands, covers her nose and mouth. She struggles to breathe, pulls desperately at the mass. She can't tear it off. The carcinoma smothering the life out of her. She struggles. Manages to stand. I watch helplessly. She careens around the room. Trays, bottles crash to the floor. A final gasp. She falls on her side, unconscious.

I check her pulse. Nothing. She's dead. The bloody splop slides off her face, slithers over to my feet, stops for a moment, slurps into the reception room, leaves a rippled blood trail.

A scream.

I dash into the room to see the receptionist trying to rip the *splop* off her face. It doesn't budge. Receptionist drops. The splop slithers down her body to the floor. Moves back to me....again. Stops…again. It oozes over my shoes, up my leg, along my arm, back into the gaping unsutured wound. It snuggles. Pulsates.

Right in front of my eyes, the incision around the splop heals as if surgery never occurred. I feel strange. Dizzy. I go to the sink, wash blood off my arm. I look at the carcinoma. It grows to twice its original size. A round smiley face appears, dead center. I smile back. Smiley face disappears.

I step over the bodies, like a bad dream. I mumble to myself, stroll out the of office, stepping over the bodies on the floor.

Me, to the carcinoma, "Well, I guess we'll have to find a new dermatologist."

M

Morgue Rat

Morty Schwartz, bottom of the Hollywood paparazzi slime pile. Maniacally accosted celebrities for the sensationalistic tabloid press. But Morty hasn't shot a sellable photo in months. Top dogs elbowed him to the rear.

Desperate. Rent, credit card payments overdue. At a loss for ideas Morty sits at Rago's bar with his only friend, petty thief, Binky Bupert.

Morty nursing a beer mutters, "I need something to shoot, Bink. Something that'll sell. Everything's been done to death."

Binky grins, "Done to death. Funny, death. Reminds me of that famous crime photographer, what's his name, from way back, the forties."

Morty, "Weegee. Right. 1940's king of corpse photos at crime scenes. Weegee said, 'Dead people are my business.' His room walls covered with corpse pix. Colleagues called it Weegee's morgue. He always tossed the dead guy's hat into the frame of his photo. Catches the human drama, makes em' more personal. People always like that human angle."

Binky, "I read once where Weegee wore a doctor's white coat to slip into the morgue and get the shot."

Morty, "That's it! That's it, Bink. Today's Weegee. That's who I'll be. Pix of dead people, not all waxed up in funeral parlor, but regular stiffs, right after they kicked. The City Morgue. Death on a slab."

Binky, a bigger grin, "And ya don't have to tell stiffs to keep still."

Morty, "How the hell do I get inside. How about you, Bink? You can pick anything."

Binky, "I...I donno Mort. The Morgue? Is shooting dead people Kosher? I don't know."

Morty flashes Bink a C-note. Bink takes the job. Reluctantly.

City Morgue cargo dock. Up the concrete steps to the doors. Padlocked. Bink jimmies the cargo door lock. Door clanks open. Rusted hinges creak. Bink's gettin' the jitters. They walk down a dark corridor. Bink's pen light is all they have. They reach the morgue elevator. Binky unscrews the call button panel, futzes with some wires. Sparks spritz, motor growls, car descends. Stops in front of them. Doors slide open. They enter elevator.

Morty jests, "Goin up."

Binky, sweating bullets. Journey's end, the morgue entrance. Bink's hands tremble as he picks the lock. Ping. Open. Bink, sweat soaked. "Th...th...this is where I get off." He runs back to the elevator. Gone.

The morgue. Quiet as a tomb. Morty's jaw drops. Face lights up. Thinks, 'Wow! Place is rolling in corpses on gurneys. Heaven.' Spots an attendant's blood-stained white coat just in case a guard peeks in. Puts it on.

Morty, overexcited, 'Party time.' Gets everything he wants, and way, way more. The whole spectrum, gunshots, stabbings, auto crashes, men, women, hot naked babes, old, young, every ethnicity, all toe-tagged with names.

Morty mutters to himself, "They're just waiting for me to give 'em their Warhol 15 minutes of fame."

Morty keeps going back. Uses Bink's pick tricks. Speed Graflex at his eye, *Click! Click! Click! Click!* Photo ops up the Wazoo. More gruesome. More is better.

Morty, in his darkroom, watching the images fade up in the developer. "Whoa Momma. Pay dirt! Look at this stuff." He scans his clothesline of drying photos. Mesmerized.

Morty, mind racing, "A gold mine. Yowzah!! You are onto something, Mortola. Go man, go."

Morty goes to see Max Pratt, photo editor, Daily News. Pratt's not real impressed. Then he spots something.

Pratt, "I know him. I know that stiff. Pasta Gatelli. Big mob boss, on rival's hit list. Finally took him out." Pratt lights up, "I'll take it." Hands Morty a crumpled twenty.

Morty gets brave. "No sale."

Pratt hands over another twenty. Morty doesn't budge. Pratt, pissed, forks over fifty more smackaroos. Morty scrams before Pratt rethinks the dough.

Pratt yells out, "Hell Morty, you could get a show with this stuff. People like lookin' at dead people."

Morty, "Long as it ain't them."

Pratt chuckles. Walks up to Morty. Hands him a biz card. "Some Wacko German *avant-garde* gallery owner, Luponais von Martin."

Morty's unsure until next day, Gatelli photo, *Daily News* front page. Sells a hell of a lot of rags. Morty daydreams, 'I'm getting hotter. A star? On my way.' Puffed, Morty goes to meet Luponais von Martin, not Martin…*Marteen*. Does his *shooby-doo*.

Marteen, eyes wide, *"Ich eine show gemachen.* I set it up."

Marteen shoves papers at me.

Morty, "What this?"

Marteen, *"Eine contract. Sei exclusive zu mir."*

Morty, "For how long?"

Marteen, *"Zein yaren*…ten years."

Morty, "You gotta be kidding."

Marteen, "Vant fame or not? *Mach schnell! Sie mir time verschenden.* Now or *noch nie."*

Morty's got no choice, thinkin', 'I wanna hit the big time.' He signs on the dotted line.

Marteen snatches contract. Makes copy for Morty. Puts original in his safe, "Gut. *Wir sind fertig,* Exclusive deal *gemachen*." They shake. Morty's hands a bit damp.

Morty thinks, 'This weirdo must be serious.'

Marteen repaints his gallery grey, "Gut contrast fur dem blacks und vites." Brashly to Morty, *"Machen Sie dem grosse, grosse*...blow dem up big, big."

Marteen slaps humongous price tags on the prints. Morty's ecstatic. Opening night, mobbed. Upper west side swells. Show sells out. Morty's cut, twenty-five grand. Morty's hot.

Marteen, "I vant *eine, eine, eine*...another show. *Gaben sie mir*...give me many more photografs de more grotesque das besser. *Schnell! Schnell! Mach schnell!'*

Morty empathetic, "Wait a minute. I took the first pictures 'cause I was broke and desperate. Now that I've made a name for myself, it feels disrespectful, not right."

Marteen, slyly, "But you must, vee haff eine contract."

Morty, "Marteen, I thought I was bad. You are nothing more than a ghoul."

Marteen, "Yah, but eine wealthy ghoul. Now *gaben sie mir mehr* photos or I will end you career, *kaput! Verstehen sie?"*

Morty caves to Marteen.

Morty, on his way to the morgue. Feeling blue. Bloom off the rose. Fame? Worth it? Is he doin' the right thing? Ruminates, 'I...I just don't know.' Lost in thought, bumps into a young chick, walking alone. "Oh, sorry, honey. My mind was..."

Girl, befuddled, "...Am I supposed to know you?"

Morty, "No. No. I just bumped..." She cuts Morty off.

Girl, "...are you Billy?"

"Name's Morty. Morty Schwartz. Famous photographer. Maybe ya heard of..."

Girl, cuts him off again, "It's very dark now. I like that."

Morty takes her in. Thinks, 'Wow! She's a real looker. Alone. I get her all to myself, nice break.'

Morty to the girl, "What's a young girl doing at the City Morgue this time a night. Not safe."

Girl, "I …I don't know. Get high anxiety. Pills don't work. Get way depressed. Coming here calms me down."

Morty, "What's your moniker?"

Girl, "No trees. Trees give me hives."

Morty, frustrated, "Ah, I mean what's your name?"

Girl, "Name? Name? Oh, I'm Alice.Alice. You can call me Alice.Alice."

Morty, to himself, 'Wha...? Alice.Alice. What? Who cares. Hot babe.'

Gets bolder, "Any chance ya'd like a cuppa java?"

Alice.Alice, "Java?"

Morty, "Java. Coffee. You up for a cup of coffee?"

Alice.Alice, "Decaf, must be Decaf. Caffeine makes me crazy."

He finds a late-night dive. They chat. Well, he chats. A monologue. Is she mute? So tight lipped. They stay late, three am.

Alice.Alice, shakes, jumps up. "I…I have to go. Go now!"

Morty, "Ok. I'll hail ya a cab."

Alice.Alice, "I have to walk. Yellow makes me nauseous. Good bye…Murry?"

"Morty…Morty Schwartz." He calls after her. "Can, I uh, call ya sometime, Alice.Alice?"

Alice.Alice, "No phone. I'm always here…like tonight…walking."

Morty, "Yeah me too."

Alice.Alice, out the door.

Morty, frazzled, "Alice.Alice, wait. I'll walk ya…"

Rushes after her. Alice.Alice vanished. Gone. Nowhere in sight. Morty sighs, "Too bad. I feel something. I like her. Wanna see her again. Definitely."

Next night after a morgue session. Morty sees Alice.Alice. "Hey, Alice…Alice. It's me Morty Schwartz."

Alice.Alice, "Do…do I know you?"

Morty, "Last night. Darby's Coffee Shop."

Alice.Alice, "I stopped coffee. Even decaf, it's still got some…"

Me, "Caffeine?"

"Yes. They sneak it in. Are you the picture taker man?"

"Yeah. That's me. Morty Schwartz." I overreach. Might get lucky,' "Hey, Alice.Alice, You could do me a big favor. I need some photos of a girl. You fill the bill. Could you come up to my place. Just for a few minutes. I take the photos, you split after. Whatta ya say?"

Alice.Alice, "I…I don't know. I have never done anything like that."

Morty, "You'll be fine. Please, pretty please, with honey on it?"

Alice.Alice, "I don't eat honey. Bugs make it."

Morty insists. She reluctantly agrees.

Morty's pad. He rushes ahead. Tosses moldy take-out boxes, beer bottles, whatever, into the kitchen. Clears dirty clothes off his couch. "Have a seat, Alice.Alice."

Alice.Alice, "No sitting, I only stand…or lie down."

Morty, to himself, 'Lie down.?A come on? Night getting brighter.' Then suavely, "Alice.Alice, would you like something to drink?"

Alice.Alice, "Water. Nice lukewarm water. Settles my stomach."

Morty give her a glass. She takes baby sips.

Morty, "So, now the pictures. Just stand by the window." Morty to himself, 'Strange, her skin has a pale blue tint.'

He shoots. *Clicks!* The clicks make her flinch. Switches to his Leica. Quieter. He snaps her every which way but loose. Alice.Alice never moves. Statuesque. Then, she just turns away, walks right past him, out the door.

154

Morty, concerned, "Hey Alice.Alice…Alice.Alice." Follows her. In the hall. Gone…again. 'Man, she's fast.'

Every time he's done at the morgue, there she is, Alice.Alice. She never remembers him. But goes wherever he takes her.

Morty and Alice.Alice. Dinner at Slooty's. She floats in. Stops. Stands. He grabs a booth. Morty sits. Alice.Alice stands, motionless. Morty hands her a menu.

Alice.Alice, "What is this, Malcom?"

"Morty. Morty Schwartz. A menu. List of food. See if there's anything you'd like."

Alice.Alice, "Can I get a bowl of lukewarm water?"

Morty, wondering, "Oooookay."

Alice.Alice and Morty are soon a couple. He ponders this strange girl, 'Movies make her brain hurt. Music hurts her knees. Knees? Strange, but who am I to judge. Not exactly playin' with a full deck myself. I…I dig her. Really dig her. Like being around her. Am I fallin, fallin…fallin…nah.'

With Alice.Alice at Phil's Bar and Grill. She refuses to sit on the stool. Stands. Morty sits. Has a beer. Alice.Alice…warm water. Neat. He downs a couple. Courage peeks..

Morty, hopeful, Pops the big one "Uh, Alice.Alice, how about you move in with me? Share my place."

She steps away abruptly, shaking. Anxiety flares. She screams, top of her lungs, hysterical. "No! No! No! No! No!! It will ruin everything!"

Alice.Alice speeds out. He follows…fast. Not fast enough. Gone…again. Where? Where?

Morty after more morgue sessions. Alice.Alice is nowhere to be seen. Gone for days. Weeks.

Binky, "You're lovesick, Morty. Feels like a bad flu."

Morty, way depressed, "Love sick? In love with Alice.Alice? I guess I am."

In his darkroom. Finally develops Alice.Alice's film. Holds it up to the safe light.

Morty, shocked, What? What? Blank! All blank! No images. The whole roll. Nothing. Somethin' musta been wrong with my Leica. Has to be it. I'll take more next time she shows up.'

She doesn't. Ever. Jilted? Morty real, real heartsick.

Marteen calls enraged. He wants another show. "Vere da hell ya been, dummkopf?. Schnell!"

Morty, "I'm just not up to it."

Marteen pesters. Morty caves. Again.

At the morgue. Morty peruses the room, thinks, 'Oh my God. Twenty-five or so corpses, all makes and sizes, smashed to pieces. Blood-sopped sheets. Blood pooling on the floor. This is too much, even for me. I almost barf. What the...? Wait a sec. The bus accident in the Bowery. Frontpage. These are the dead passengers. I want to get the hell out the place. I'm torn. Marteen's voice echoes through my head, 'I vill destroy your career.'

Morty stays. Slowly pulls back bloody sheets on the mutilated corpses. Clicks slower, slower. Stops. Sighs deeply. Gingerly raises his cameras. A soft tap on his shoulder. Startled. He turns. It's Alice.Alice...totally nude.

Morty yells "Alice.Alice! What the....."

She puts finger to his lips, "Shhh". She points to an open morgue drawer, whispers, "This is why I can't move in with you Marvin."

"Morty Schw..."

Alice.Alice cuts him off once again, "This is my home. My drawer. These people are my family."

Morty, too loud, again, "Your...your family! These dead..."

Morty too himself, 'I must be dreamin, nightmare.' Slaps himself. Alice.Alice is still there, naked.

Morty still loud, "You don't mean you're...you're..."

Alice.Alice shushes him again.

He whispers, "You're...?"

Alice.Alice, "Six months. Some brain thing. Probably a bad movie."

Morty, "But you look so normal."

Alice.Alice, "I got sent to a funeral parlor by mistake. Shot full of formaldehyde. That's why I'm so well preserved." She points around the room. "I live here."

Morty, double shocked, "You *live* here?"

Old lady pops from under her sheet. Gruff whisper, "Quiet please, mister. Respect those who have passed."

One by one, all the corpses sit up. Man with half a face, hissing softly, "Yeah, you heartless scum bag."

Lady with no arms, "Making money off the deceased, shameful."

Morgue Guard peeks in. "What the hell you doing here? Hey, you're the sicko takes dead pitchers. Saw the write-up in the news. You better come with…"

Morty, real loud now. "Look at 'em. All alive, sitting up. Something's not right."

Guard, "Yeah, you buddy. These stiffs ain't gonna move anywhere, asshole. You drunk?"

Morty turns. All the corpses are down, sheet covered. Alice.Alice's drawer shut.

Guard, "You better come with me, buddy. Breaking, entering's a felony." Walks toward Morty, cuffs dangling.

Morty make a break for it. Knocks the guard down. On the street, running, bumping. Crazed. Out of control. Morty stumbles down the subway steps. Head spinning. Hears the din of an oncoming train. Pushes thru the crowd. They push back, knock him down onto the tracks.

Morty, deer in headlights. *Slam! Squish!* Morty no more. 'Then why am I still thinkin'?'

Accident area taped off. Cops shove back rubber necks.

Alpha paparazzi slips cop a fin. Aims camera down on the tracks, freaks, "Hell, that's Morty Schwartz. The *Morgue Rat.* Made it big takin' pix a dead people. Now he is one."

The morgue attendant wheels Morty in. 'I'm dead? Morty Schwartz, dead?'

White coat covers Morty with a sheet, attaches ID tag to Morty's toe. Leaves.

Silence…then, Alice.Alice's drawer slides open. She steps out, floats over to Morty's gurney. Real sad face. "Oh my poor, poor Maurice. Look at you. A mess. What happened?"

Morty answers, head plopped on his chest, "Got pushed onto the subway tracks. Mowed down by the Lexington Express. I feel terrible."

Another voice. Eyeless dead guy sits up. "Yeah, feels like that in the beginning. You get over it."

Alice.Alice tries to put him back together. Does the best she can.

Morty, "It's so great to see you again Alice.Alice. You ran out. Broke my heart." Struggles to his feet. Hugs Alice.Alice. This time she hugs back. Leans in, kisses him on the lips.

Morty kisses back, his arms, such as they are, around her. The group croons, "Awww!!!!"

Morty turns, sees everybody, everybody. Sits up, smiles at them.

Old Woman, "You two make a fine couple. Best of luck. I get burned up in the am."

Morty, shocked, "Burned?"

Alice.Alice, "Cremated. No living relatives, you get Potter's field."

Morty, "Guess I'll be there too."

Alice.Alice…smiling broadly, "Us, together, Morty."

Morty, Gleefully, "You remembered my name."

Alice.Alice, "Things are different now. Morty Schwartz."

RIP Morty and Alice.Alice. RIP.

M

Ice Box
with
Art Lasky

What do I mean, you might ask? It's always mindless zombies with the occasional skulking ghoul thrown in. Here I stand right before your eyes, and still... What do you think? No, don't answer; you see a zombie—don't deny it. Am I mindless? Rotting before your eyes? Sneaking? Shambling? Skulking? No, no, and no. Not that we want notoriety. We're better off slipping by under the radar. We are clever, careful, and completely unknown. There is not even a name for our, shall we say, species. Perhaps you can come up with a name before—

But I get ahead of myself. There is time yet, let me tell you how it all began:

Imbedded memory. The Ice Box. I'm six. The year is 1951. Ice box. Ubiquitous, rectangular, white slab against the kitchen wall. Two doors. Top. Bottom. I love ice day. The iceman cometh. A massive block of ice between rusty tongs rests on his shoulder. Grandma opens the top door. The iceman slides the block in. Cold food for a week. I follow him out to the alley, his truck stacked with ice. He picks me off a chunk. Smiles. I smile back.

A big day. Our first refrigerator. Movers put the ice box on the back porch for the junk man. We all stand in awe in front of this big, white machine. Dad plugs it in. It gets cold, food goes in. No more iceman. No more ice blocks or ice cubes. I'm kind of sad.

Out on the porch playing, I stop, stand at the ancient ice box. Get a bad idea. I open the bottom door, just big enough. I slide in close the door. *Thunk!* It's dark. Too dark. Quiet. Too quiet. Had enough. I want out. Feel around for handle. There is none. Outside only. I panic. *Scream! Scream! Scream!* Nobody hears. Insulated, isolated. My knees cramp. Painful. Keep screaming, nothing. Hard to breathe. Gasp. Choke. Dizzy. Sleepy. Then...nothing.

Rickety old junk truck, brakes screeching, comes to a stop at my back yard. Junk men get out, and climb the porch steps. Pick up the ice box. I'm still in it. Heart beating? Barely. Junk men drag the ice box out into the alley where I played with the neighborhood kids. No more, I guess.

They throw the icebox on the back of the truck. Rumble away. The rumble stops. Junk yard. Junk men heave ice box into a pile of discarded ice boxes. Heartbeat stops. Ice cold. Forever.

Evening. Fading light. One by one ice box doors open. Rotting boys and girls slough out. Now. The young walking dead.

It's getting near dinner time. I thank you for the company. As you may have guessed, my friends and I prefer our meat raw, fresh...alive. You will scream, cry, and beg. Do not worry though, nothing you do will disturb our feeding.

"Come on gang. Dive in."

They do. *Gnaw. Rrrrip. Chew, chew, chew. Gulp. Slurrrp. Yum.*

M

Comatose

On the third ring he picked up.

Lou, "Lou here."

Sotto voce, "Ah, Louella Darnell, grifter and con artist par excellence—my star pupil. You dropped off the radar fast."

Lou, "Yeah, the Lexcorp gig went sideways. Who'd have thought the accountant was an honest man?"

Voice, "Honesty. What a racket."

Lou, "Thank god there are so few."

Voice, "Amen beautiful, AMEN!"

Lou, "So, what have you got for me?"

Voice, "And here I thought this was a social call."

Louella's laugh was sexy, musical. "What's more social than separating marks from their money?"

"True dat....Just so happens I've got a couple of irons in the fire. One of them is perfect for you."

Lou, "I do like perfect."

Serious, "Here's the sitch. CyberCorp, data retrieval outfit. CEO Dennis Prattner. Weak spot, addicted to secretaries. Goes through 'em like jelly beans. Looking for a new squeeze, computer/business savvy and above all an easy conquest."

Lou, "Oh, I am oh so easy," she purrs."

"He won't like the price he pays... but that's the easy part for us. Let me work my magic. I'll set up an interview."

Two weeks pass. Lou prepares for her lunch interview. She dresses for lunch seduction interview. Donning her 'do me' duds. Dolce Gabbana ultra-short, low cut black silk dress, single string South Sea pearls, Jimi Chou black satin heels, Stella McCartney black silk blazer, Clive's Dragon. Out the door. Limo.

Dennis Prattner, good looking, Harrison Ford type, tailored suit, red power tie. Sees Lou, drools.

She gives him her bogus CV, Ph.D. computer science from MIT; MBA at BU; BS in Public Relations, Cornell…all "verifiable". *Grifters anonymous* covers her ass.

Dennis buys it hook line, yada, yada, Hired, vetted, bedded.

Lou screws his brains out. She muses as he humps away, *'Schmucks never learn. Do not shit where you eat. Always a big time pay back…big time. Always!'*

Six months later she's top VP at CyberCorp and Denny's mistress. Total access to the company finances. Lou thinks about her next steps, *'Maybe stay in one place for a while. Keeping one jump ahead of the law, exhausting. She could snuggle right here in CyberCorp. She still needs a safety net, in case her plans go south. Dennis always misplaces his cell. Dummo Denny.'*

Lou proclaims loudly, "That'll work!"

Assistant, leans through her open office door, "Did you call me, Miss Darnell?"

Lou, "No, just happy thoughts out loud. Oh, before you go…where is Mr. Prattner?"

Assistant, "I believe he just left for lunch with Mr. Barron, Chairman of the Board."

Lou, "Perfect, thanks."

Lou heads to Dennis's office. His secretary doesn't even look up when Lou lets herself into his empty office. Used to seeing Lou as a frequent visitor. Secretary keeps her head down, especially when Mr. Prattner orders her to hold all calls while he's 'meeting' with Lou.

Sure enough, Dennis Prattner's phone sits forgotten on his desk. Lou downloads names, numbers, sex-selfies with ex-mistresses. Lou smiles, *'Is he that dumb, or that arrogant? Whatever. My insurance policy's secure.'*

Lou's apartment, a few nights later. Insurance policy comes into play, sooner than Lou expected. Dennis arrives late for their dinner date. Rushes in.

Dennis, "Can't stay long, babe, but I gotcha a little present." Tosses her a two-gram vial of cocaine. "Merck. Pure as silk."

Lou smirks, "Is this a Dennis consolation prize for a quickie? In, out, bye-bye Lou-Lou?"

Dennis, "Shake it, Lou, I got a restaurant reservation. Alma's birthday."

Lou, "A date with wifey-poo. How sweet."

Dennis, "Just get your ass in the bedroom."

Bedroom. Denny sits up, way pissed. Post coital confab. "What the hell are you talking about? Full partner? I made you."

Lou, "I made you more, lest you forget a pending billion-dollar merger with Cryptodat. Closes in two days. You'll make a bundle—hell, two bundles. Take it public. That deal is my baby. I made it all happen."

Denny vaults out of bed. "Forget about it. Lou! It's my company! I'm the sole CEO... period!"

Lou, "Maybe this birthday present for Alma might change your mind." She holds up her cell photos, a slew of his selfies with his hookers.

Lou, devilish grin, "Family portraits."

Dennis, "You tapped my cell?"

Lou, "Names, addresses, cell numbers included...free of charge."

Denny yells, "Gimme that damn thing, now!" Jumps onto the bed. They wrestle. Lou breaks free, slips off the other side. He chases.

Dennis hisses, "You bitch. I moved you to the top. This is how you pay me back?"

Lou, "Not if I get what I want."

She laughs her ass off, waving her cell, trapped in a bedroom corner. No escape.

Lou to herself, *"Shit. I overplayed my hand."*

Lou holds up her cell. "Back off Dennis, or little Alma has the worst birthday ever."

Denny's fast. Grabs for Lou's cell, but not before she hits send. Denny pulls the cell from her grasp. Drops it on the floor. Stomps it with his bare foot. Nothing. Picks it up. Hurls it against wall. Phone shatters, but Lou's download to Alma is already done. Dennis picks up a massive metal ash tray. Closes in. Blood in his eyes. Too fast for Lou to escape...again. Clocks her on the side of the head. Stars. She falls. Denny, demonic, grabs Lou's head between his hairy hands, and slams it on the edge of her glass coffee table. Crack!

Lou thinks, *'I feel weird. Cold, head to toe. Not right. Out cold...am I dead? No, I can see... and hear.'*

Denny rages, "Come on bitch, I'm not buying your possum act."

Denny kicks her. Nothing. Panic replaces anger. "Blood! Oh my God so, much blood...Shit! She's not breathing."

He pulls off Lou's neck scarf. Grabs bloody ashtray. Wipes off his prints. Drops ashtray on Lou's head.

Dennis, "I'm outta here...serves her right." Uses Lou's scarf to turn the doorknob. Lets it float to the floor. Out and gone.

Later, Denny home with wifey Alma, sipping martinis. Cell rings.

Dennis grabs the cell. "Yes, this is Dennis Prattner. What? Oh my god! Is she still alive?"

Dennis freaks. Ashen. Cold sweat. "Yes, doctor. Thanks. Please keep me informed."

Alma, "What was that all about? You look like death warmed over."

Dennis, "Police found Louella in her apartment. Unconscious. Signs of a struggle. Head injury. Cocaine everywhere."

Alma, "Cocaine?"

Dennis, "Lou was into it big time. Likely a run-in with one of her low-life dealers. Who knows? Secret life. A lot of guys. I kept her habits under wraps. The doctor said she was in some kinda pseudo-comatose state. Damn! Couldn't have happened at a worse time! We're supposed to finalize a merger with Cryptodat this week. She did the deal. It's all in her head. With her down, I'm dead in the water."

Alma, "Louella's life is more important than some darn deal."

Dennis, "Not some deal. Billion-dollar deal. Puts us over the top. I can go public."

Alma, "Your righthand woman is in trouble, and all you think of is business. People first, Dennis. People first."

Dennis, "Yeah, yeah, right of course…people first."

Alma, "You should go see her now."

Dennis, "I'm…I'm too upset. I need a drink." Goes to fridge. Takes icy vodka bottle. Pours a glass. Downs it.

Alma, "I'll go with you, for moral support."

Faint lightning flash. The muted boom of distant thunder.

Denny, "Big storms brewing, heard warnings on the radio. Dangerous driving conditions, heavy winds. Monsoon rain."

Alma, "You're not made of sugar. You won't melt. Let's go, before the storm hits."

Hospital room. Lou, head in bandages, hooked up to an array of machines, slowly becomes aware. She hears machines beep and hum. Faint buzz of voices. She opens her eyes, sees Dummo and Alma chatting with a man in a lab coat. Lou, to herself, *'Doctor? Damn I can't move. Sweet Jesus! I'm paralyzed in a hospital bed.'* Lou focuses on the doctor's voice.

Doctor, "There's a chance she'll live, or..." Lightning flashes. Loud thunder, close, cuts him off. Lights flutter, go out.

Doctor, "Everyone stay in place. Power outage. Emergency power will kick in."

Lights blink, on, off, then on again. Then stay on.

Doctor continues, "She has brain damage. She may be able to hear and see, but not speak or move. It can last hours, days, go on forever, or lapse into a full coma, possibly brain dead."

Lou, *'Brain dead, great. Number one on my bucket list.'*

Alma, "Poor dear. Such a lovely woman."

Dennis frowns, "Yeah, lovely."

Kaboom! Terrifying lightning strike, shatters windows, fire ball crashes into the room. White hot, zig-zag bolt splits in two. *Zig zaps* Alma! *Zag zaps* Lou! Bodies convulse. Alma drops into her chair, head droops forward. Eyes shut tight. Nurses rush into the room. Machines go *Ping! Ping! Ping! Ping!*

Lou to herself, *'What's happening to me.'*

Her monitor buzzes and vibrates. Vital signs decline. Monitor display loops chaotically.

Lou to herself, *'My head's pounding, throbbing, so much pain. Aw, shit. Sayonara.'*

Monitor flat lines.

Doctor, "She's gone."

Alma, feeling strange, 'Gone but not forgotten, Dummo.' Stands up abruptly. Shaking. Her eyes pop open, sly whisper.

Dennis, "What'd you say?"

Alma, "Me? I didn't say anything."

Dennis, "I could have sworn I heard you say...forget it. Let's get going."

Doctor, "Sorry for your loss."

Dennis, "You're sure she's dead?"

Doctor nods and walks over to Alma. "I should admit you. That was quite a jolt. You could suffer..."

Alma, "No! I'm fine doctor, just fine." Straight and tall, like nothing happened. In control. "Thank you for your concern, Doctor. We'll take care of Lou's funeral expenses."

Denny barks, "What?"

Alma, "She wants to be cremated. Ashes to ashes...the least we could do."

Denny, "Jesus, Alma. You're talking crazy, Maybe you should be admitted."

Alma, forcefully, "I said no! I mean no! Let's get the...heck out of here. Now!" Alma struts out of the room. Denny follows. Bewildered.

Denny, Working late.

Alma home alone in bed asleep. She bolts upright. Wide awake.

A voice in her head, *'Where the hell am I?'*

Alma, freaks. "What? Who said that?"

Lou, *'OMG. I'm in Alma's head.'*

Alma, out loud, "If there's somebody in my house, I'll call the police."

Lou, to Alma, *'I'm in your head, not in your damned house. Me. Louella Darnell. Something weird happened. The lightning bolts. My mind jumped...into yours."*

Alma, trembles mumbling, 'This is crazy. Get a grip on yourself Alma.' She slides out of bed, weaves into the bathroom. Goes to the sink, splashes cold water on her face, slaps herself. 'Wake up, Alma, wake up...please wake up.'

Lou, in Alma's head, *'You are awake. Wide awake. We're in your head... together.'*

Alma, terrified, "This can't be happening!"

Lou, *'Can't be, but is. Now do us both a favor. Sit on the john. Quick before we pee on the floor.'*

Alma plops. Pees.

Lou, *'Ahhh, thank god. I was about to burst.'*

Alma stands. Glances in the mirror, freaks out, loud, "My eyes. They're bright blue. My eyes are...were... brown."

Lou, an accomplished grifter, adapts fast and runs with the ball, *'No more, kid. You've got my baby blues. They jumped over with me. It'll wear off by morning.'*

Alma, "I'll call Denny. He'll...he'll..."

Lou, *'Sure, call Dummo. He'll be a great help. If you get your damned cell phone this will make a lot more sense.'*

Alma, "Denny was right. I'm out of my mind."

Lou, *'Go get your cell. Now. Before you do flip out.'*

Alma, "I'll go downstairs and call him."

She skitters down the steps clinging to the railing, swings into the living room.

Lou, *'Sure. Great. Call whoever the hell you want. Call 911. Let 'em take you to the funny farm. I'll come along for the ride. Look, Alma, I can prove this. Remember when we first met? Denny's men's club. New Year's Eve? Last year?'*

Alma, speechless.

Lou, *'You were wearing a yellow and white shirtwaist. We chatted about the gold broach you had around your neck.'*

Alma shakes her head, incredulous.

Lou, *'Your mother gave it to you when you graduated high school. It belonged to your beloved grandmother, Mum-Mum. That's what you called her.'*

Alma, "This is nuts. That's it, I am nuts."

Lou, *'Okay, remember the wine stain on the mattress a couple of months ago?'*

Alma, "Yes. Hey! How did you know about that? We fired the housekeeper."

Lou, *'Too bad. I made the stain, we were trying a little something different in bed, your bed—the stain was shaped a little like Texas.'*

Alma, "No one else knew about that. Sweet Jesus, Louella... is this really you?"

Lou, *'Bingo, you got it. Now button your lip. All your loud chatter's getting on my nerves. We can talk quietly right inside your little noggin.'*

Alma, "Heaven help me. You are in my head. I can think you."

Lou, *Finally. That was exhausting. Got any vodka? I need a drink.'*

Alma, "Denny keeps a bottle in the freezer."

Lou, *Well, Alma baby, let's get it.'*

Alma to kitchen. Gets freezer bottle. Fills a nice big water glass half full.

Lou, *To the tippity top, dear. Let's sit at the dining room table. Bring the bottle.'*

Alma sits.

Lou, *Bottoms up.'*

Alma, "I …I don't drink."

Lou, *Ya do now.'*

Alma grimaces, "It's so strong."

Lou, *Come on now, girl…glue, glug, glug.'*

Alma, "Oh dear. I never knew it tasted so…so…"

Lou, *'…damn good?'*

Alma, "Yes, yeah…damn good."

Lou, *Makes ya feel…?'*

Alma, "Damn good!"

Lou, *Now yer talkin. Grab your cell. Best take another coupla swigs. You'll need it.'*

Alma drains the glass.

Lou, *'Ok, now open up the photo app and feast your new baby blues on these.'*

Alma, blown away, "It's…it's… Denny…and you. you're…you're…"

Lou, *'Screwing the livin daylights outta your cheating hubby. Keep going.'*

Alma, "Another girl? I've got to sit down."

Lou, *Next.'*

Alma, "Two girls at once?"

Lou, *'One's a hooker.'*

Alma, "Black stockings, garter belt?"

Lou, *Whatever turns your Dummo hubby on. Proceed.'*

Alma, "How many…"

Lou, *'Four that I know of. He'd been at it long before I came on the scene. This next one's my personal fav.'*

Alma, "How did they get into that position?"

Lou, *'She's a contortionist. Yoga teacher.'*

Alma, "That...that chubby blond...with a penis."

Lou, *'Dildo, fake rubber cock. Strap on. Denny's in the blond wig. Gender swap."*

Alma, "What does she do with that...dildo thing? Never mind. Forget it. Too much information."

Lou, *'Here's the headline. Dummo's the one who put me in the hospital.'*

Alma, "He said you had a fight with a drug dealer."

Lou, *'Total bullshit. I told him I wanted half the business. Equal partners. He went ballistic. Hit me. I fell. He grabbed my head, slammed it on the corner of my glass coffee table. He totally freaked. Dummo thought I was dead, but I could see and hear. He rubbed coke on my nostrils. Sprinkled the rest over my face, put the empty vial on the floor, crushed with his heel. Called 911...split. Dummo thought he murdered me.'*

Alma, "He's...he's...he's... a...a......"

Lou, *'Go ahead, say it. Nobody here but us chickens.'*

Alma, "...a murdering bastard! I'll divorce him."

Lou, *'Not near enough, Alma Baby. Not anywhere near enough. Dennis Prattner's gonna get pay back big time.'*

Denny home from work. Opens front door. There stands Alma, in a sexy low-cut dress, black stockings, high heels. Dressed to kill. Ice cold martini in hand.

Denny, "Damn Alma. You look so...so..."

Alma, "Delectable?"

She hands him the cocktail. "Down the hatch, baby."

Dennis gulps. She throws her arms around him. Long French kiss. Breaks.

Alma, sultry, "Next stop, bedroom."

Lou, *'Alma, you go girl! You got him huffing and puffing. Screw him like a hooker.'*

Denny, dazed, "Alma…that's…that's…that's…"

Alma, "The best sex you'll ever get."

Dennis, "Where'd ya learn those moves?"

Alma, "Yoga class."

Denny turns to get his usual apres coitus smoke. Alma pulls out a hypodermic needle, jabs full thrust it into Denny's thigh.

Dennis yelps, "Awl! What the hell was…?"

Alma, "*Apres* sex cocktail, honey. Propofol, Thiopental, Protobarbitol. Nighty night, Denny."

Dennis, out cold. Alma on her cell, taps 911.

Denny in a hospital bed. Three doctors beside him. Doctor one, "Pseudo-coma. Idiopathic. Oh, sorry, that means cause unknown."

Late night. A nurse enters Denny's room, checks his vital monitor. Leaves. Moments later another nurse enters the room, a white purse over her shoulder. It's Alma. She takes a tube from the white bag, squeezes large bead of electrolytic gel into her palms. Rubs hands together, takes wooden tongue depressors from the pockets, places them between her teeth, bites down hard.

Lou, *'Piece de resistance, Vipertek's VTS-989 high voltage taser, twenty times what cops use.'*

Alma gingerly removes a small black box from the purse. Red button on the side, sharp metal prongs on the back. Alma rips open Denny's gown, smears on gel, whams the taser on Denny's hairy chest.

Lou, *'Set timer for two minutes.'*

Alma complies, then tapes it in place, and grabs hold of Denny's hand. Presses the red button. *ZZZZAAAAPPPP!!!!* Taser's mega jolt travels through Denny to Alma. Both shake spasmodically. Alma plops into her chair. Head drops. Eyes shut. Denny, eyes spinning.

Denny, in Alma's head, to the girls, *'What the hell's going on. What are you two doing here?'*

Alma, *'We thought you'd enjoy a brain-to-brain visit from the women in your life.'*

Lou and Alma erupt in a rant of vitriolic babble. Denny, powerless, speechless.

Alma delivers the goods, *'News flash! Dummo. DataCorp merges with Cyberdat, goes public. Reaps billions. Info, Courtesy of L &A Datafem, Inc. New moniker for Louella and my conglomerate.'*

Denny, *'You...you can't ...'*

Alma, *'Done deal, ex-hubby. So long asshole.'*

Taser timer beeps, then...*Zzzzaaaapppp!!!* Alma stands up, back to normal. Flips Dennis over. Takes another hypodermic from purse. Pulls up Denny's gown exposing his fat rosy-red ass.

Lou, *'Nail em, kiddo.'*

Alma stabs it into Denny's ass with a vengeance.

Alma, *'Parting shot, bastard. Sleep tight.'*

Denny's eyes close... slowly.

Lou, *'Fait accompli, sister.'*

Alma high fives herself. Starts out the door. Turns back, blows Dennis a final kiss.

Girls, in harmony, *'Bye, bye...Dummo.'*

Dennis Prattner, body on ventilator wheezing. Comatose.

M

Wake Up!

Willy McFarlen dropped dead in Rowdy Pub after his eighth tumbler of whiskey. He was the most-loved and most-hated man in all of County Cork, Ireland, but never had a problem luring a gaggle of drinking buddies, lads and lasses, to hang out, opening and closing every pub in the Cork. Favorite beverage, *Dublin Dark Whiskey*, the costliest blend.

Willy's wake is a grand affair. His house was packed with those he loved and those he loathed. Laughing, crying, cursing, and most of all getting drunk.

Archie Martin, Willy's best friend. Archie's shapely wife, Violet. They walk over to Willy's coffin.

Violet, "He looks so calm, so peaceful."

Archie, "Not like the lively Willy, always kickin' up a fuss." Arch lays his hand on Willy's chest. "Good heart, sotted head."

Violet, "But always sweet to the ladies."

Archie, "And then some."

Violet leans in and plants a kiss on Willy's cheek, hesitates, then kisses him full on the lips. A might too long. Pulls away.

Archie, pissed, "Why the hell did ya kiss 'im on the mouth?"

Violet, blushing, "I...I don't know. Did I?"

Archie, grim, shakes his head, mumbles, "Women."

Timothy McAlester, loudly, "Wonder what ol' Willy'd say if he knew we were drinking his special whiskey."

Room suddenly quiet. Very strange at an Irish wake. Willy sits upright in his coffin. The crowd gasps.

Mortician, Bilbo Rattleford, "That's not possible I shot him full of embalming fluid meself."

Willy, still sittin' up, "Land o' Goshen, Bilbo, I've drank more anti-freeze than that stuff ya pumped in me. And I walked away."

Willy scowls, "And to answer Timmy's query, I don't feel too keen at ya'll sloshing down those two cases o' me Dublin."

He sprightly hops out of his coffin, leisurely leans on it. Guests drop-jawed. Still.

Willy yells out in his McFarlen growl, "I love ya'll and hate ya'll, but there's two here I never told me true feelin's. Truth Number One, Archie Martin. I've hated your fat ass since fifth grade when ya stole my girl Lauralee MacKennen from me, just when I'd cooed her into a hand job."

He strides up to Archie, SMASH!!! A quick, strong right-handed coldcock to Archie's jaw. He drops on his fat ass, wobbles to his feet.

Archie, "But, I'm your best friend Willy."

Willy, "No matter."

Gives Archie another right, then a hard left, a gut punch and knee to his family jewels. Arch, down for the count.

Archie grovels from the floor, "Ya broke me nose, ya bastard."

Arch's bulbous schnozz, blood running like a faucet. His wife Violet quick to help him.

Willy, "Truth Number Two, My undying love lust for Violet Marten, nee Lillywhite."

Archie burbles through a torrent of blood, "My God man, Violet's been me wife of fifteen years, bore me three young Martins."

Willy, "No matter. I was never bold enough to declare my pining love for Violet. It's stronger than life itself. Hell girl, I never stopped loving ya through my own marriages." Nods to several women, they nod back. "May the Lord bless all of ye putting up with this son-of-a-bitchin drunkard. But

180

Violet...dear Violet was and is my only true heart's desire. And... I mean ta make it right tonight."

Willy prances up to Violet, grasps her hand. "Off we go lassie."

He pulls her up the stairs. A door slams. A quiet moment...then mattress thump!, thump! thump!...on and on. Backed up by an ever-increasing crescendo of passionate screams, "Oh dear God, Dear Jesus, my savior, thank you! Thank you, THANK YOOOO!!!"

And that was Violet.

Willy hoots, "Ooohwee girl, ya drained me dry. Another go?"

Violet, "If ya got it in ya, loverboy."

A repeat, more cacophony the second time around. Then simultaneous, "AHHHHH's...OHOO, OHOO!!! EEEKK!!! YES, YES, YES", again, and again. Even the guests below became exhausted.

Rustling, bustling sounds. Then four feet hurry down the steps. Violet straightening her bodice and dress. Willy finishin' belt bucklin'. The pair waltz into the living room. Violet's twinkling starry-eyed daze, her beaming lighthouse smile, along with Willy's deedle-dooin' and a bit of Irish jjggin' tells the tale. Willy twirls Violet over to her husband Archie, bloody kerchief held up to his nose.

Willy, "She's mine now, fat ass." Willy sloops over to the table, picks up an unopened quart of Dublin, cracks it, pulls the cork. Puts to his mouth and by God, Glug! Glug! Glug! Glug! Glug! Drained the whole damned bottle.

Willy, "Ahhh, yes. That's better. Friggin' gives a man a mighty thirst." He grabs a tumbler full of booze, raises it high, "And here's a final toast ta all ya bastards and bitches in me life.....and death. Farewell."

He drains the tumbler, then smashes the glass into the fireplace. Abruptly, Willy grabs Violet's hand, nods, smiles. She nods, smiles back. They scoot over to the coffin. Willy helps Violet up, tumbles in behind her.

Archie red-faced, frozen.

Willy, "Ya won't be hearin' no more words from us tonight. Drink up ya dolts. He reach's up pulls down, slams coffin lid shut. Bam! All are shocked by Violet's squeals of pleasure floating from the coffin.

Archie gets his nerve back, runs up, opens the lid where the sated, placid lovers lie in embrace.

Willy's eyes pop open, wide frown. He jolts upright yelling, "Close the damn lid ya dummies, give us some privacy."

Willy pulls coffin lid closed. It momentarily rocks and shakes. Violet's giggles of pleasure fly out. Then both, in unison, "Ahhhhhhhhah" Then silence.

Archie sits weeping in a chair, Willy's empty whiskey bottles strewn around his feet. He slugs down a bottle's last drop, totally smashed as only a heartbroken Irishman can be.

Archie stands, shakes his tightly closed fist at Willy...and Violet's coffin, yells, "Ta hell with ya both..."

...I pray to God neither of ya cuckholds ever, ever, ever...wake up."

M

Gene War

I see Emily, my almost fiancé, dash from the kitchen to answer the ringing phone. Always cheerful.

"Hello," she answers. Then grim, "Just a moment, I'll see if he's free."

She covers the mouthpiece. "Allen, It's…it's her. Your ex. You want me to…"

Me, "No, it's ok. I'll handle it, but stay here, baby, I'll need your moral support."

Me, on the phone, teeth clenched. "Brenda, you were told never to call me again. Restraining order. Remember?"

Brenda, "I want something."

"What would I ever give you after what you did? I found you in my house…"

Brenda corrects me, "Our house."

Me, "Screwing my best friend in my bed."

Brenda retorts, "Our bed."

Crazed, I yell, "So what the hell do you want?"

"Your sperm. I want your sperm," she asks, nonchalantly.

My face gets red hot, "What!"

Brenda, almost whining at first, "Larry and I, …well… we want to have a baby. Start a family." Then, gathering a head of steam, "My God-given right. American dream. House, car, family."

I freak, spit words into phone, "You're a certified mental case. Use Larry's damn sperm!"

Brenda, not backing off, "He's…infertile. Bar fight. Some guy kicked him in the jewels."

Me, adamant, "Who would want to father your baby? You're a lousy, traitorous shit. You smashed the windows in my Porsche. You painted graffiti on my garage door. On top of that you took a shit on my front steps."

Me, on a roll, "You were a schizophrenic on a psych ward. How did you get out? I could never sic you on a child. You'd probably eat the baby. You're a maniac. I do not want you anywhere near me."

Brenda, "Ditto, turd face." Mood swing, sweet talk, "Be kind. For old-time's sake. Imagine how incredible my child would be. Your looks and my brains."

Me, "Your brains. Is that a joke? I'm a top lawyer in a top firm. You majored in ergonomics at a junior college. You sell grotesque furniture."

Brenda, "I run ErgoFirm. I design green furniture."

Me, "You went bankrupt. Twice. You're the joke of the ergonomic industry. This conversation is over."

Brenda, sounding confident, "Hold on asshole. You're forgetting something."

Me, "What could that possibly be?"

Brenda, "I haven't signed the divorce papers yet."

Me, "Blackmail? Is that what your delusional mind is scheming?"

Brenda, "Call it what you want. Your lawyers ripped me to shreds. Left me with nothing."

Me, "You're right about that. The court found you adulterous. End of story. You got what you deserved. Nothing. Case closed. Go to a sperm bank."

Brenda, pleading, "I want to know where my child's genes come from."

Me, "You got a whole country club of guys to screw. If they ever let you in the door. I've got a new life. A new

186

relationship. A wonderful, loyal woman. I'm out of the picture."

Brenda, "Think so ass face? You screwed me out of everything. My turn to screw you."

Me, "No, you screwed yourself when you screwed Larry."

Brenda, "Pay up, shit brain. You want me to sign? I want your genes. Listen close, dimwit. You don't give me what I want. I will make your life a living hell." Click!

My brain reels. Brenda's capable of anything. She needs to be committed, again. Maybe I can talk some sense into Larry. Hopefully Brenda's boyfriend has a shred of sanity.

I drive to her house. Park where she can't see me. Watch her slum outside, dressed in a black floor-length dress. Morticia on a bad hair day. Lights one cigarette another. Gets in her ancient Chevy. Leaves for work. Work? Brenda? A sick joke. She sits waiting for nonexistent customers. Bankrupt. Repossessed. No inventory.

Strange, Larry's car's still in the driveway. Hasn't left for work. Get out of my Porsche, windows replaced, walk to the front door. Unlocked. I enter. Larry on the floor, unconscious. Vial of Halcion on coffee table. I slap him awake. I find cold coffee sitting on the stove. I force it down his throat. He comes around, gradually. Untie him. He can't stand. Lies there weeping.

Larry rants, voice slurred, "A madwoman. I...I...ta...ta...ta told her I ha...ha...ha...had enough. Gonna leave her. Drugged me. Tied me up so I couldn't desert her. Screams she needs me. Needs a child. Child needs a father. She's psychotic. Homicidal. Never takes her meds, she drinks a fifth of vodka a day, pops Dex like jellybeans."

I watch Larry. Wonder what Brenda's going to do next. She's capable of anything.

Larry's parting words, "Watch it, Allen. She's out for blood." Wobbles outside. Struggles with keys. Unlocks the door. Falls onto the car seat. Cranks the engine, revs up, speeds off, open driver-side door swinging wildly.

'Out for blood.' Larry had said. Then it hit me. Holy shit. Emily. She's going after Emily. My god, I drive maniacally to my house. Rush in. Emily, out cold, lying on the floor. Nose bleeding. House reeks of gasoline.

Brenda, hiding in the shadows, steps out, wild-eyed, gun in one hand, gasoline can in the other. Turns and faces me.

Brenda gestures to Emily. "She's not dead. Yet. Gonna die in a blaze with you. In my... my house...if I can't get what I want, your whore won't either. No one gets your genes. French fried."

Brenda moves towards me. Gun poised. Emily wakes. Sees it all. Screams, top of her lungs. Brenda, distracted. I lurch. Grab her gun hand. We struggle, careen around the room. She breaks away. Holds the gun on me. Starts for the door, yells as she stats to leave. "Love to stay, watch you sizzle, but..."

Crunch! Emily smashes a bronze sculpture on Brenda's skull. Hands go limp. Gun and gas can drop to the floor. She sinks to her knees, quivering. Gasoline spills—plut pluts out of the can, seeps around her.

Brenda, crazed, "Damn, I need a cigarette." She pulls a pack from her pocket with one hand, grasps the lighter with the other. Plucks a cigarette with her lips, raises the lighter.

Me, panic-stricken, screaming, "Brenda, Brenda, no, no!"

Brenda, hisses back, "No? What, fart breath? I told you the deal."

House ignites. Adrenaline rush. I pull Emily out the front door, top speed. Make it to the lawn.

Brenda, human bonfire, stands in the doorway, screeches, "They are mine. MINE! I will be back!"

Stops, drops, burns. Her tortured voice rants, "MINE! MINE!"

CACOPHONOUS BOOM!!! Throws us to the ground. House disintegrates, Brenda incinerates.

Genes saved...unless...nah, not possible...but... a voice echoes, *"I will be back!"*

M

Obleah

New Orleans Police Precinct 51.

Police Officer Wayne Braggart, Wayne Braggart, a massive cop driving a squad car. His partner Smoochie Mumford, a skinny asthmatic, addicted to his inhaler, rides shotgun. Whoosh. Another puff.

Smooch, "This stuff's gonna kill me."

Braggart, "Something will. Nobody gets out alive. Pull over here."

Smootchie nudges the curb. Braggart gets out. "Stay in the car. I got business."

Smootchie, "Window shopping, Brag?"

Braggart grins, "Groceries."

Smootchie laughs. Coughs.

Braggart walks up to Minky Toper, well known street hustler. "So, Mink, what ya carrying? I need a plant."

Mink, "Jesus Sergeant, that's three this month. Ya givin' em away?"

Braggart, "Button it pal, while you still got teeth."

Mink, "I...I got nothing. The Skulls bought me out."

Braggart grabs Mink fast. Slams him against the brick wall.

Braggart, "I told you to stop selling to bangers."

Braggart raps Mink hard upside his head. Minky falls into a line of garbage cans. "You're my stash. Mine, mine only. Get it." Braggart leaves Mink on the ground. Living garbage.

Braggart lounges on the precinct steps. Takes a last deep drag off a cigarette. Flips the butt at a ratty stray dog. Dog whines. Scrams.

Braggart grins, walks into the station house yelling, "Smootchie! Get your ass out here! Smootchie!"

Desk Sergeant, "Smootchie's out sick. You got a new guy, Officer Jahson. Just up from downtown."

Desk Sergeant calls, "Officer Jahson?"

Jahson, "Yes sir."

Desk Sergeant, "Over here."

A young black officer walks over to Braggart. Extends his hand. Braggart does not shake. Turns away fuming.

Braggart leans in close to Desk Sergeant. Harsh whisper, "You stuck me with a spade rookie?"

Desk Sergeant, under breath, "Cool it, Braggart. You already got five grievances. Suck it up. You'll have your Smootchie kissin' your butt soon as he's sober."

Braggart fumes more. Powerless.

Desk Sergeant hands him a fax, "Here's the sketch of the suspects in the Whitney's drugstore robbery. Two boys in hoodies. Faces blurry."

Braggart snatches, scans. Mumbles audibly, "It could be any hood…" Bites his tongue…"body in the district."

Desk Sergeant sternly, "Try to bring a suspect in…alive…for once."

Braggart smirks, "That's up to him." Storms out calling to Jahson, "Move it rook. Ain't got all night."

Jahson rushes after Braggart.

Desk Sergeant shakes his head, mutters, "Friggin animal."

Braggart off duty. Civvies. Stops at a lamp post for a smoke. Pulls a pint of rye from his hip pocket. Butt in one hand. Booze the other. Drains half the bottle.

A frail, old black woman, with long, white dreadlocks, slips out of the dark. Calls out, "Braggart!"

He instinctively pulls out his snub-nose .38 street gun. Spins. Sees the woman.

"Careful dread head. Almost bought it."

Woman, "Hear you're looking."

Braggart, "Whatta you know?"

Woman, "Everything."

Braggart, "Skip the jive, Hag. What are you talkin'?"

Woman, "Something perfect...just for you."

"Braggart, "You a runner?"

Woman, "I get what is needed."

Braggart, "Got it on you?"

Woman, "I'm old, not crazy. Come to me tomorrow night."

Braggart, "Where?"

Woman, "Treme. Esplanade."

Braggart, "Address?"

Woman, "Just say *Obleah*. They know."

Braggart stares as she is engulfed by the night. Holsters his piece. Shakes his head. Walks on.

Braggart and Jahson in squad car. Braggart, snide, "Turn here...newbie."

Jahson, curt, "Officer Jahson, please."

Braggart, snide, "Whatever...rook."

Jahson frowns, slight head shake.

Braggart, "Pull behind that mess a Rastas."

Jashson rolls cruiser to curb. Braggart gets out.

"Stay here...rook. I got business." He saunters down the street, up to the Rastas.

Sneers, "Hag. Obleah?"

Guy shrugs, "Never heard of her."

Braggart grabs him by his jacket. Pulls close. "Easy or hard, raghead. Your call."

Man, unshaken, smiles, points, "Basement. Red door, Officer Braggart."

Braggart, "You know me, rag?

Man, "All know you…Officer."

Braggart throws him off. Strolls over to rickety steps. Walks down. Hand on holster. Thumps closed fist on the red door. Nothing. Thumps harder. "Open up…it's…"

A small window opens.

The old woman's face fills the frame. "Ah, Braggart."

"Officer Braggart to you, old witch. Open the damned door or I'll open it my way."

Locks clank. Door rattles. Old woman swings it open. Braggart enters. Old woman smokes ganja in a marble chillum.

Braggart coughs, "Jesus, I'll get wasted just from your stinkin' fumes. Let's get this done."

"Of course, Officer Braggart."

The woman walks to a small altar with a porcelain gold crowned black lion, a symbol of *Rasta Messiah, son of God, Jah."* She kneels. Bows head. Tokes. Smokes. Mumbles. Reaches behind Crowned Lion. Pulls out a small pearl-handled silver revolver. Braggart drools. Grabs It. "A beauty. Perfect. Made to order." Slips it into his boot.

"Like a glove. Damage?"

"Real silver. Hundred."

"Hundred? No damn way."

"Ninety, no lower."

Braggart, wry chuckle, "I forgot ta tell ya Rasta Momma, today's my birthday. Ya just gave me my first present. Don't bother singing. I'll just make a wish."

He blows out altar candles. Sarcastically sings, "Happy Birthday to me…" as he leaves. Slams door shut.

Woman goes to the altar. Relights candles. Kneels. Exhales a smoke plume over the gold crowned lion. She smiles, "Now it begins."

Braggart and Jahson, night shift, cruising New Orleans Lower Ninth. Poor. Black.

Braggart spots two young men in hoodies.

Braggart, "Bingo, rook. Pay dirt. Pull over." Leans out window. "Whatta you hoodies up to? Coming home from a party?"

Braggart, "Names. Tall first, then Shorty."

Tall, "Whasup, officer? We didn't do nothing."

Braggart, "That's for me to know. Ain't it? Names. Now!"

Tall, "Tray-Tray."

Shorty, "Pitbull."

Braggart, "Wise asses, huh." Gets out of the car. Shines a flashlight in Tray-Tray's eyes. "Real names, real quick...or in you go."

Tray, "Bernard...Willis."

Braggart, "And you doggie."

"Fernando Lader."

"Live?"

Bernard, "Holy Cross."

Fernando, "Same hood. Next door."

Braggart shoves the fax next to Fernando's face. "You look a lot like this guy who hit Whitney's. Where were you Tuesday night, around nine?"

Bernard, "Playing ball. Jamison's lot."

"Witnesses?"

Fernando, "Lotsa dudes."

Braggart shakes fax, "You gotta admit, it does look like ya."

Fernando, "Could be anybody."

Braggart, "Tru dat. All you spades look alike."

Bernard, "That's racist, man."

Braggart backs hands Bernard. Spins him flat on his back. Fernando lurches to help him up. Braggart kicks him. Lands next to Bernard.

Braggart, "Look at that. Pair of spades. Good poker hand."

Fernando grabs Braggart's leg. Pulls hard. Braggart topples off-balance, goes down on one knee.

Bernard to Fernando, "Run dude. Now!" Fernando, mouth bloodied, takes off.

Braggart's faster. Grabs Fernando's hood, places boot on Bernard's neck.

Braggart, venomous, "You picked the wrong dog in this fight, pickaninnies. Cuff the spades, rook. Assaulted a police officer."

Fernando, "You assaulted us first."

Bernard, excruciating pain, "Get your boot offa me. I'm choking."

Fernando, "You're breaking the law. Don't you watch CNN?"

Jahson, "Let him breathe, Braggart. It's policy. You damned well know it."

Braggart sneers at Jahson, "Looking out for your little brothers, rook?"

Fernando, "Besides...it ain't us. Playing ball. Remember...Officer?"

Braggart, hissing, "It's you because I say it's you."

He lifts off his boot. Momentary distraction. Fernando breaks away. Runs. Braggart fires. Misses. Gone.

Braggart, "Go after him, rook."

Jahson doesn't budge.

Bernard struggles to his feet, gasping. "You ain't gonna get away with this, pig."

Braggart, crazed, "Oh, but I will." *Blam! Blam!* He shoots Bernard in the chest. Bernard drops.

Jahson, "Braggart, you just killed an innocent man."

Braggart, "He attacked me. Pulled out a gun. You're my witness, rook."

Jahson, "There is no gun."

Braggart reaches into his boot. Takes out the silver revolver. Puts it in Bernard's hand.

"There is now."

Jahson "You can't do that..."

Braggart grinning, "Policy?"

Jahson, "They'll bring you up on charges."

Braggart, "Not if they don't know, and…now, he's a cop killer."

Jahson, "What?"

Braggart, "He killed a cop."

Jahson, "Cop…what cop?"

Braggart, "You, rook." *Blam!*

Braggart shoots Jahson in the head with the little silver gun. Down he goes. Braggart kneels, plants little silver gun back in Bernard's hand.

Squad car pulls up. Two officers, jump out, flashlights beaming, move to the scene.

Squad policeman, "Neighbors heard shots."

Braggart, "Captain Ross. Just in time. Two bangers. Hoodies, matched the fax. One got away." Gestures calmly to Bernard's body. "That one tackled me. Pulled out a gun. Still in his hand. Shot Jahson. I had no choice." Points, "Jahson's over there."

Captain, "Jahson? Who the hell's Jahson?"

Braggart, "The black rook the Desk Sergeant stuck me with."

Captain, "We don't have any rookies in the precinct. You signed out with Smootchie."

Braggart, "What are you saying? …this rookie… Jahson…the spade…"

Officer Kent flashes his light. "There's no gun in the suspect's hand, Captain." Jerks light up to suspect's face. "Holy shit it's…it's Smoochie. Braggart shot Smoochie."

Braggart freaks. Goes to body, "Smootchie? What the hell? Something's not right. It was the banger. He shot…"

Office Kent, searching for Jahson's body. "There's nobody here."

Braggart panicked, "I saw him fall. I saw it."

Captain, "I think you should come with us back to the station, Braggart."

Braggart spins, confused, eyes wide, mouth, agape, blank face. Mumbles, "...little silver gun...the little silver gun I...I..."

Captain, "Kent, take his piece, get his badge. Cuff him."

Click! Metallic rasp echoes. Braggart handcuffed. Catatonic.

Obleah kneeling, praying to *The Lion*. Door creaks open. There stands Jahson in shadow, dressed in black. Obleah stands, walks to him. Kneels at his bare feet.

He says three words, "It is done." Hands her the little silver gun.

She bows, whispers, "Lord. Son of Jah."

He places hand on her head, says, *"The lord hates hands that shed innocent blood."*

Backs into the night. Gone. Obleah stands, drifts to the altar, places the little silver gun behind Gold Crowned Lion. Kneels. Takes her chillum. Fills with ganja. Lights. Deep drag. Her head raised high, eyes closed, blows thick smoke, through the cloud, proudly—

"Rasta Justice."

M

Enigma

with
Rebecca Perrin

I bolted from sleep in a panic, my shirt soaked with cold sweat. It was not a dream that woke me. I never dream. My anxiety was unbearable. My long years as a psychiatrist may have helped my patients but gave me little insight into my own crisis.

Two and a half years ago I came home late to find my wife, Lucida, lying on the living room floor. Her head resting in a pool of blood, a gun in her hand. My gun. I knelt beside her. She was still breathing. I called 911.

The dispatcher said, "Stay calm, help is on the way."

The EMT arrived, applied a pressure bandage to the wound, strapped her in the gurney, and wheeled her to the ambulance. I followed close behind as the EMT, drove her to the Deerwood ER, siren blaring.

I wondered why in god's name Lucida would try to kill herself? Especially now. She had everything to live for. Excited to have made full partner in the law firm, Lewis, Cohn, & Brantley, a devoted mother of two teenage girls, Wendy and Laura. We were best friends, dedicated, in love, a solid marriage. It made no sense. Not Lucida.

In the waiting room, I paced, a knot in my stomach, dreading news of her condition.

A young doctor pushed open the ER doors and came up to me. "Your wife has serious brain damage. She's in a coma. It's doubtful that she'll ever regain consciousness. Even if she does, she will be severely mentally impaired."

I felt dizzy, nauseous, not comprehending his words.

I was at Lucida's bedside every day for months. Her condition never changed. One evening, leaving her room, I was stopped by Detective Wayne Canter, flanked by two uniformed policemen. Wayne had been my patient. Beating his struggle with alcoholism made us close friends.

Grim faced, Wayne said, "Allen, forensics found your fingerprint on the gun trigger. I have to take you downtown. You're under arrest for attempted murder."

I pled innocent at the trial. My attorney was Harry Closell, a very dear friend of Lucida's. But he could not explain away the hard evidence: my gun, my fingerprint, and the prosecution claimed I had motive—money. Lucida's death would have made me the sole beneficiary of a ten-million-dollar portfolio she had inherited from her father.

The jury found me guilty. The judge, John McAllister, another of Lucida's admirers, slammed down his gavel. "I sentence you to forty years. I'd give you life If I could."

Sitting in prison for months after the incident, I faced an appalling dilemma. Lucida's living will had appointed me proxy if she was ever in a vegetative state, her current condition.

My fate was hanging in the balance. Lucida was the only eyewitness to what had really happened that night. Though I had been in prison thinking about it for months, I still had no clue who had a reason for killing her and setting me up. I was the accused. She was the victim. Taking her off life support would end her life. The prosecutor would charge me with first degree murder. This was a death sentence state. I was in was a no-win situation. Innocent, but nowhere to turn.

I received a letter from Wendy. "Dad, we're coming to prison see you."

I knew what they wanted to talk about. There was no delaying it anymore. When the girls arrived, Laura blurted out as soon as I sat down. "Dad, you can't let Mom linger like this."

I was surprised that Laura had come. She had refused to talk to me after my arrest.

Wendy scolded her, "Damn, Laura, give him a damned minute." Swearing was new for Wendy but she did it well. She was a daddy's girl.

"Listen, Dad," Wendy said. "You know the portfolio you got from Mom's death? Put it into what's called an Irrevocable Living Trust. Make Laura and me the trustees. That way you won't benefit from Mom's death. We will. You'll be in the clear. It would show you had no motive."

What was she talking about?

"I've been taking an AP business class. I talked to my teacher. This will work, Dad. It's all taken care of. I retained a lawyer. He'll messenger you the trust documents and the papers giving your consent for Mom to be taken off life support. All you have to do is sign them."

My God, Wendy has grown up in two years.

Silent until now, Laura whispered, "Wendy and I will be there with Mom when she…at the end."

Laura stood up to come to me. I broke down, holding nothing back.

Wendy caught her sister's hand, pulling her down on the seat. "Daddy, there's something you need to know."

"No, Wendy, don't!" Laura cried.

Wendy leaned toward me. "Mom was having an affair with Daniel from the law firm."

I felt a sharp pain in my chest.

"She was going to leave you. She was lying to you," Wendy continued.

Laura's face flooded with tears. She murmured, "Wendy wiped the gun down. She didn't know one of your prints would still be on the gun. I didn't say anything at the trial. I didn't want you to know about Mom. I didn't think they would convict you."

Sobbing and shouting at the same time, Wendy spoke, her face crumpling, "I knew how much it would hurt you! You loved her so much. But she was going to divorce you! I couldn't let her do that. I used gloves so no one would know who did it."

I went numb and slid to the floor.

Wendy shrieked, "You didn't deserve what she did to you, what she was going to do! I did it! It was me. I had to kill her."

She pulled a gun from under her dress, put the barrel into her mouth...

I screamed in horror, "No! No!"

Laura tried to stop her. Too late.

"Blam!"

Case closed.

M

Exquisite Corpse

With
Corrine Sherer

Now, if I knew where we were, why wouldn't I just say so?"
The woman slid her white Lolita sunglasses to the top of her
head. The sun had fallen quickly anyway, dropping into the
horizon like a pink egg. She looked at the man in the driver's
seat, her husband, with an impersonal chill.

"To piss me off? Make me drive around like an idiot? How
should I know what goes on in that head of yours?"

The man's eyes did not leave the road. They were fixed
and hard as dimes beneath his brow.

"Do you really believe I'm that petty? My god, George, do
you think I *want* to be lost out here, God-knows-where, after
dark?"

"You're right, Margaret, sorry," George began.

"Thank you," she said with a gesture of exasperation.

"You're never able to resist an opportunity to tell me how
wrong I am so you can act superior," he sneered.

"Oh, brother," Margaret laughed sourly. She kicked her
canvas sneakers onto the wide dashboard of the Plymouth.
George drove on in silence. Margaret lit a cigarette and looked
out her window, past the dark trees, and onto the coarse edge
of the violet Oregon coast. She rubbed at goosebumps on her
tanned legs, exposed in her short, gingham jumper.

George sighed. Margaret turned to him expectantly. He
looked at her and sighed again.

"Marge, it's just that you embarrassed me back there. And
at the office picnic. For God's sake…"

209

"It's not my fault that boss of yours wouldn't know Tibet from Tijuana. I had to correct him. I mean, what a blowhard."

"Marge…" He began, and then allowed a small chuckle. "I know, right? And geez Louise, all those yes men just sitting there nodding along like a bunch of shmucks."

He ran a hand through his short, coiffed hair. A few locks gave way and were blown across his forehead by the cold night air.

"Well, so much for that map, huh?" Margaret pulled it onto her lap again and squinted over it.

"I can't see a damned thing but we're still driving south, right? The water's been on my side the whole time so that makes sense."

"Don't we need to go east?" George lit a cigarette, beady and bright red in the dark car.

"I mean, a little east, but more south, no?" The pause hung between them. "Do you think we've gone too far?"

"I don't know, Marge. Maybe." He stops "Look, over there."

He motioned towards a figure ahead of them. A pale flag, a hitchhiker's thumb, was extended out to them.

"No, George, let's not. I've already got the creeps being out here."

"But maybe he'll be able to give us some directions. Come on, let's pick him up."

"All right," she relented with hesitation.

Suddenly the car accelerates, smashing right into the hitchhiker, making a sound like a watermelon dropped off the top of a skyscraper.

"Oh my god George, you ran over him."

"I floored the gas pedal instead of hitting the brake. It was an accident." George shrieked.

"Well, get out and help him," Margaret orders.

George gets out of the car and walks to the front. "Damn, his head is under the front tire. He's…he's dead. Smells gamey."

Margaret, more sympathetic, "Probably homeless. Just needs a bath."

"Not anymore. Clothes from the dollar store." George adds,

Margaret barks, "Since when are you a fashion expert, dimwit. You have to back up."

George, "But I'll run over him twice."

Margaret says, "Just get in and back up. We can't leave him under the car."

"Could you get out and direct me," George asks.

Margaret slips out and stands by the car. George starts it up. The car lurches backward.

Margaret shouts, "Hit the brake! You're cutting him in half. For crap's sake. Just go slower."

George inches cautiously.

Margaret shouts again, "Stop! Stop! Idiot! That's far enough. He squirted all over my new jumper. You know how hard blood is to wash out."

George, feeling hopeless, "What do we do now?"

Margaret answers, "Call 911."

George frantically searches his pockets. "I can't find my phone."

Margaret says, "Use mine. It's in my Vuitton handbag."

George rummages through her bag. "I can't find it."

Margaret, "Dig deeper."

George, victoriously, "Got it."

He dials. Nothing. "No bars. Out of range. No signal. Please get in. Let's get out of here."

Margaret, officiously, "It's against the law to leave the scene of an accident."

George argues, "No one will find out."

Margaret, confused, says, "Don't be stupid. The car's covered with blood, and...and other stuff."

George panicking, "I'll wash it. Just get in."

Margaret peers closer, "I can see his wallet. It's halfway out of his back pocket. We should at least find out who he is... I mean was."

She bends down to get the wallet. "I think I'm going to vomit."

George begs, "Please get in the car. Let's go."

Margaret stands up. She gags, holding the blood-soaked wallet by her thumb and finger, like it was a dead mouse.

"This is gross," Margaret mutters. She opens the wallet, pulls out the license, reads 'Gerald H. Winkelmeyer'. Dumb name." Turning the card over. "He's an organ donor. Not much left to donate. We can't leave him on the road, cut in half, with a squashed head. We'll do this. You take half, I'll talk half. We'll put him in the trunk."

George squeamish, "I am not dragging half a man to the trunk."

Margaret, impatient, "Just get out and do it."

George, jitters out, shuffles over to Margaret.

"Pick up his left leg," she says methodically.

George bends down lifting the leg. He stands motionless.

"Get moving!" Margaret says.

George closes his eyes, sliding his half to the back of the car.

Margaret struggles. "Mine is too heavy for me. Come here and help."

George, losing it, "This is...is insane."

Margaret, pissed, demands, "Just help me."

George and Margaret tug the right half of the body to the trunk.

Margaret says, "Open it."

George pops the lid, "My golf clubs are in here."

"Numb skull, take your goddamn clubs and get rid of them."

George, grasping the golf bag to his chest, gazing down at his prized possession.

"George!" Margaret calls out.

He jumps, gently placing his precious clubs on the roadside.

Margaret, matter of factually, "You take his shoulder, I'll take his foot."

Bending over, she breathes deeply, "On three. One, two, three, oof."

They heave the body half into the trunk, then do the same with the other half.

Margaret, in charge, says, "Close the trunk. The smell is disgusting."

George slams the trunk lid. Covered in blood, he starts to cry. "I...I can't believe this is happening."

"Get your act together sissy." She walks to the car door. Gets in. "Hurry up, we have to finish this."

George gets in the driver's side. "Finish what?"

"Getting rid of it...him." She calmly unfolds the wrinkled map.

George, whimpering, "How are we going to do that?"

"Just drive, dunderhead. Something'll turn up."

They pass an old cemetery.

"Jesus, look at that. Now it's getting creepy."

They hear an urgent banging coming from the trunk.

A muffled voice pleads, "Stop! Stop here."

Freaked, George slams on the breaks. "What...what do we do now?"

Margaret says, "We get out and see what the hell's going on in the damned trunk."

George whines, "You...you go. I'll...I'll stay..."

"Get your lazy ass out, useless."

They both get out and open the trunk, cautiously.

213

George gags, puts his hanky to his nose. "Smells like rotted meat."

Boing! The body's head pops up, says, "How would you smell after spending four months in a wooden box six feet under?"

Bottom half leaps out, helps top half onto its waist.

Body says, "There, much better. So, this is my stop, thanks for the lift."

This human disaster walks up the hill, nonchalant, steps into the cemetery.

Margaret swipes her hands, clean, "Well, that's that."

George, frozen with fear, speechless.

Margaret glances at her Tiffany watch, "And we still have time to get to the club for a night cap. You're sick. I'll drive."

She opens the door slides in on the driver's side, starts and over revs motor. George is standing beside the car, frozen, like a statue.

Margaret, fed up, "Get the hell in, douche bag, or we'll be late."

George slowly clumps to shotgun side. Gets in, catatonic.

Margaret, ready to party, "I seriously need a double."

Margaret peels out. The car disappears into the night.

"What a weird couple," the corpse mutters, to no one in particular.

M

Climax

James Smelter, 29, tall, handsome, sits staring intently at his laptop. A rising star with Consolidated Fracking, USA's biggest oil producer, his assignment, debunk progressive movement *Climax*, i.e., *climate change*, phrase becoming a useless cliché, changed to *Climax* by lame progressives. Millions of bumper stickers printed until the dim *left* realized the double entendre. Laughingstock. Sex sells. Humiliating.

James drives his brand new Beemer to his way cool Soho loft, parks in a no-parking zone, puts a fake government employee free parking card on the dashboard, locks up, smirks. Takes the elevator to the fifty-seventh floor. Enters key code, strolls inside. Sleek furnished pad. James slips off his tailored suit coat, rolls up his sleeves and scans his email. Whoa! A message from *Loveless Lonelies*, his favorite online scoring site. He signs in. Pix of Gail A. blips onto the screen, long blond hair, killer blues…drop dead gorgeous. James, intrigued, sits at his desk.

Gail A. texts "James, I was hoping you'd respond. Your bio was intriguing."

James, smugly, "Glad it caught your gorgeous eyes."

Gail A., "Would you be interested in having lunch this week? Discuss common interests?"

James, "Of course, Gail. My lunch hour is 12 to 1, any day."

Gail A., "Tomorrow? There's a place near me that has good food, *Happy Health*, Corner of 14th and 1st. Noon ok?"

James, "Got it. Look forward to meeting you…Gail."

Gail A., "I'll be wearing a yellow daisy in my hair, so you can recognize me."

James, staring at Gail A's screen image, "Oh, I'm sure I'll spot you."

Gail A., "Great. See you then. Have to sign off. Work beckons. Goodbye...Jimmy."

Gail A.'s photo blips off. James shouts, "Yes!" Fist thrust in the air.

Lunchtime next day. James finds himself in a low rent, rundown neighborhood, scans the store fronts, sees a dingy window sign, *Happy Health*, grimaces, crosses, enters. Door screeeeeches. Gnashes his teeth. Place empty. He sits, looks at the filthy table, hands primly up, snaps his fingers at a long-haired kid in a dirty apron behind the counter uncurling a fly paper strip.

James, "Excuse me, but could you wipe off...this table."

Kid, "Holy Moses. Musta missed that one, be right there."

James checks his cell, 12:00 exactly. He moves way back, yuk-faced, as the kid wipes the table with a grimy rag.

Kid, "There ya go, sir. Spic and span."

James picks up the tacky plastic menu. It crackles as he pries it open. "Jesus," he grunts. Loud door screeeech. Teeth gnash...again.

James, to Kid, "Ought to get that door oiled. Damned annoying."

Kid, no reaction.

James head-jerks as a young woman walks in. Black straggly hair streaked red and green, nose ring, lip ring, earrings, arm tattoo whale spouting, torn tee shirt graphics, *Climax Sucks*. Ultra-short skirt, fishnet stockings, knee holes, black high-top sneakers, way too much black mascara, snapping chewing gum. Kicker, a large daisy stuck in her coif. Her nasal voice cuts the silence like a buzz saw.

Gail A. "Hey, Jimmy-boy...that you?"

"Yeah, James Smelter, and who the hell are you?"

"Gail A., *Loveless Lonelies*, last night, remember?" She struts over, pulls out a chair turns, it backwards, straddles. Leans in.

Gail A., "Nice ta meet cha in the flesh, Jimmy."

James, frowning, "No way. I saw the picture. Definitely not you, sweetheart."

Gail A., snotty, "How da ya think I'd look after you guys raped the hell outta me?"

James, "You were gang raped. When?"

Gail A., "Name the time, Jimbo, eons is my best guess."

James, out of character to show concern, "Where?"

Gail A., "Here, there, and everywhere. Beatles, cool tune."

James, "Holy shit. Did you call the cops?"

Gail A., "Useless, just another bunch a you guys. So, ya gonna stay or go, your call, Jimmy? Hungry?"

Gail A. waves at the counter boy, "Hey, Benny-baby, large algae, kombu, smoothie."

Turns to James. "You, Jimmy?"

James, "Just water…bottled, wipe the bottle."

Gail A. whips the menu open. "Not hungry, Jimmy? All vegan. My fave, seitan dogs, faboo."

James, "Is there any real food on this menu?"

She yells to Benny, "Benny boy! Give my new friend a Yak cheese veggie burger with gluten-free fries."

She jumps in before James can speak.

Gail A., "Cool bio. Fracking, huh? No windmills or solar for you."

James, "Nope. Gas and oil dwarfs alternative, hundred to one."

Gail A., "This one breaks me up…electric cars."

James, "Me too. Still need fossils to generate juice to keep them going, and gas guzzlers still dominate."

Gail A., "Don't matter where you guys stand, left, right, middle, whatever, you guys love your creature comforts. You guys never learn."

James, "Learn?"

Gail A., "Supplies run out."

James, "Not in my lifetime."

Gail A., "So short-sighted. What about your offspring?"

James, smirking, *"Their* problem. I won't be there."

Gail A., "Me first, me, me, me. You guys are so hardwired."

James losing patience. "What's this *you guys* crap?"

Gail A., "I'm not part of your clique."

James, "Clique? What the hell does that mean?"

Gail A., *"Species* is more like it. Lean in real close Jimmy-boy. Time to start the presentation." Gail A. writes in the air with her black-nailed index finger. The words *Homo $apien$*, appear in gossamer cloudy letters.

Gail A., "...$apien$. *You guys.* Get the picture?"

James, slack-jawed, on his feet. "How the hell ...?"

Gail A., "Dollar signs, cute, huh?"

James, "I don't know what the hell is going down, but I'm outta here." He tries to move. Feet frozen. "This is crazy. Who the hell are you?"

Gail A., "Stay with me, Jimbo."

She air-writes again, speaking along, "G...A...I...now lose the 'L,' end with...'A'. *GAIA*, shimmering neon rainbow."

James, "Gaia? What the hell kind of name is that? You lied to me."

Gaia, "My real name. Been around a long time, keeping my eye out on...*you guys.* Unfortunate accident. Slipped on a mossy rock near a scummy pond. My hand skimmed the surface. *ZAP!* Your relatives left the pond, kept the scum. Pay attention, Jimmy-boy."

Gaia snaps her fingers. *Bling!* They are surrounded by dense jungle, swarming with exotic animal life.

James, "Where the hell are we?"

Gaia, "Rainforest."

James freaks, "This...this is a dream. A nightmare. Wake up, man, wake the hell up."

Gaia, "Yeah, 'wake the hell up'. Been trying to get you guys to do that since you discovered fire. Look around. Cramped, overcrowded, not much left after you chain sawed your way through. Never know what the hell can fly out."

Gaia snaps again. A once pristine ocean beach glutted with foul detritus. water birds, crude oil soaked in death throes.

Gaia, "Wanna take a swim, Jimbo? Catch." She throws him a towel, devilish grin. Snap! Nothing but endless ice.

James pulls up his collar, freezing.

Gaia, "See that pool of water? Your precious island city prime waterfront, give or take, ...whenever. PowerPoint over. I gave you a gem, you took a dump on it. Your bad."

James fearfully, "Me?"

Gaia, "Hell no. All a ya. Done deal." *Finger snap!* Jimbo's body ephemerates into a void. Nothing. And all his kind. Gaia smiles, "Evolution glitch. I shoulda stuck with the lizards."

M

Lawn

♫ *Green, green, green,* ♫
♫ *greener, greener, green,* ♫
♫ *your lawn craves,* ♫
♫ *"TruGreen" supreme* ♫.

If I see that friggin' tv commercial, with its absurd dancing cartoony grass tufts, giant eyes, gianter mouths, screeching that damn TV jingle. Disgusting...and I work for that company, *TruGreen Lawn Fertilizer Corp.* Harry Moorcroft, Head chemist at the place, fifteen years. Ignored. Bored. Try to get the old fart, Brandon Rigerly, owner, into R&D, make *TruGreen*, truer green. He's a lazy, rich thief. Stole the original TG formula from an old, destitute botanist, Philby Rigerly, by chance, his second cousin twice removed, who died penniless. Brandon, on the other hand, raked in millions due the phenomenal success of *TruGreen Lawn Food*, consumed tonnishly by every true American male, obsessed with lush, green front yards, competing rabidly with neighbors also addicted to ♫ greener, ♫ greener, ♫TruGreen green lawns.♫

I should just quit, start my own damned company, make my own bundle. So...I do. Quit I mean. No bundle yet, but my new formula will put TruGreen outta biz, sending that crappy tv jingle into the ether.

I work maniacally after hours in my basement lab, failure is not an option. Dogged, I push on night after night, then it comes to me in a dream. Dried animal blood. A monster nitrogen rich plant additive I blend, half and half with purloined TruGreen. I sprinkle freshly seeded test pots. The results, encouraging. The pots sprouts grass blades, less than a week. I know I can do better. To hell with *dried* blood. The real thing, purchased from a local slaughterhouse. Way better, but I'm going for stupendous. How? Dunno. Blocked. I pace, consume more than my quotient of Haig, *fortuitously*. A drunken accident. I slip on an errant garden slug. *Squish!* Lose my balance, drop my booze glass. Shatters on lab table. I grab the edge to keep from falling. Ooopsy. Palm into glass shards. Slice! Deep lash, squirts blood everywhere. Panic. Spin. Search, for a cloth to sop the bloody torrent. Unwittingly, blood drenches seeded test pots. I wrap a dish rag around my hand, drive to ER. Get sutured. Back home. Boozy, woozy, crash on the couch.

Morning, way overhung. I schlog to the lab. Eureka. I found it. Flabbergasted to see blood-stained test pots bursting forth rich green blades, six inches overnight, no sunlight. Unheard of. My fresh blood nurtured my babies. Hell, obviously can't merch this fertile blend using my own hemoglobin. A person can barely live, drained of two quarts. I'm driven, not suicidal. Aha moment! Medical supply firms' market whole blood to hospitals Google search. A grand a pop. No matter. Victory in reach, I go for it. Use my old *TruGreen* credentials. Buy four liters. Way over budget. Can't stop. Spread my new blood rich formula over my lawn. Two weeks, growth so dense I need to mow twice a day. Not even the most fervent lawn dude would go for two mowing's per diem. I cut the dose. Perfect. Formula down pat. Christened, *"HumaGrow."* Unfortunate reality check. Costs a hundred bucks a bag. No buyers, no how. Drawing board. A solution will manifest. Always has. Haig tumbler. Sleep on't.

Takes three cups of espresso to get me moving, then…light bulb! Bright idea! Darwin Menacer school chum. School creep. Darwin runs a budget funeral parlor. Always up for a deal. We do lunch. He agrees but wants a cut 50-50. Deal breaker? Deal breaker. Cuts too deep into my goal of banking a million ASAP. Another dead end. Funny, dead end. Resume brainstorm. Look out my bay window. Damn! My ultra-lawn needs cutting. If I don't do it today, rain expected tomorrow. It'll be a jungle, three, maybe four mower passes. I dawdle. Noon, blazing sun. Sunshine. Another lawn booster. Now or never. I slather SPF 50, don a hat, attack my beauteous beast. Who knows? Mayhaps a plan will surface. I cut, cut, cut. Mowing. Sweating. Thinking. Mowing. Sweating. Thinking. Nothing. Yet. Then…something I heard on my car radio sifts mindfront. A plea. *"Help the homeless, help themselves."* The homeless. The friggin homeless. Arm thrust. *Yes! Yes! Yes! Help the homeless, help me!* This glorious new plan puts vigor in my mowing. Finished. Exhausted. Strip, skinny dip, my pool. Sluice out dripping. Refreshed. I lay on my lush, soft, ultra-lawn warm sun drying me. It reverberates in my mind, Help the homeless…help the homeless…help…I drop off to dream of the millions my new improved *HumaGrow* will reap.

Awake suddenly. Something weird. Try to sit up. Cannot. Can't stand up. No way. What the…? My eyes peer down to my feet. Terrifying visage. Am I still asleep? A nightmare? No, this is all too real. Slithering grass tendrils creep up, around, through me. My arms, legs, neck, torso. Can't yell. Gasp for air, as my pet lawn pulls me into the ground. Under the ground. Ingested. Digested.

Weeks pass. Lawn untended, unwatered, unfed. Dead. Brown. Save one patch, healthy thriving, curiously in the shape of a reclining human. The patch stayed green for months. Harry fed his lawn well.

♫ *Green, green, green,* ♫
♫ *greener, greener, green,* ♫
♫ *your lawn craves,* ♫
♫ *"TruGreen" supreme.* ♫

227

About the Author

Mick Benderoth is a New York filmmaker, TV commercial director, screenwriter, and rock & roll musician. He spent twenty years in Hollywood as a screenwriter before returning to New York to direct television commercials. Mick now resides in Manhattan, NYC, writing and publishing fictional prose. Mick's book *Flix: Clips from a Filmmaker's Odyssey* is available on Amazon and Kindle. For more information, visit MickBenderoth.com.

www.ingramcontent.com/pod-product-compliance
Lightning Source LLC
Chambersburg PA
CBHW030615250626
47154CB00014B/979